PRAISE FOR

Victorian Stillness

"Kip's distinctive writing style breathes vibrant life into both characters and settings, crafting an immersive journey that took me on an emotional rollercoaster. From moments of pure delight to heart-wrenching dismay, this award-winning author delivers a definitive five-star experience."

—NATACHA BELAIR, Award-Winning Author of
A Stellar Purpose

"With a lyrical intensity, Kip Langton evaluates the acidic impact of greed, entitlement, and manipulation on a quiet sense of place and belonging. Through characters that are complex and riveting, Langton creates a narrative that unfolds step by step to a conclusion that is both challenging and uplifting. Using a touch of mysticism, a wellspring of understanding of our collective impulses and flaws, and a powerful command of the music great writing can create, Langton has crafted a book in *Victorian Stillness* that is to be savored and reread."

—GREG FIELDS, Award-Winning Author of
Through the Waters and the Wild

"*Victorian Stillness* shows the complex nature of property, tradition, and responsibility. A true masterpiece, Langton showcases his artistic and creative natural ability throughout the entirety of the novel."

—EMILY KEEFER, Author of *The Stars on Vita Felice Court*

"In the footsteps of the great American storytellers, a new voice emerges: Kip Langton is one part Harper Lee and two parts John Irving. Langton deconstructs the American family unit and its values, leaving us with bittersweet humor and pathos in its wake."

—ALEX SPAK, Executive Creative Director, Publicis Worldwide

"The best psychological fiction book I've ever read—the new *Empire Falls*."

—JON KOSTAS, CEO of Apollo Pact

"Step into a world where the peculiar meets the commonplace, where characters both bizarre and relatable reside in a microcosm of life's intricacies. This book is a vivid exploration of the universal within the specific, offering a unique and captivating journey for readers."

—NICOLE PATRICK, Actor, Singer, and Influencer

"Delving into the human struggle—a book about a place you've never been to but have always known. An American epic packed into a simple story about a declining property in upstate New York. A tragic, yet inspiring warning for us all."

—JACLYN LAWRENCE, Licensed Master Social Worker

"More visual than a painting. Cinematic all the way through. You can't stop until it's done. Then you're left with the mood it has created. It stays with you, like a song stays with you. Few books do this."

—M. H. WRENN, Painter, Mechanic, and Fisherman

VICTORIAN STILLNESS

Victorian Stillness

by Kip Langton

© Copyright 2024 Kip Langton

ISBN 979-8-88824-277-3

All rights reserved. No part of this publication may be reproduced, stored in a retrieval system, or transmitted in any form or by any means—electronic, mechanical, photocopy, recording, or any other—except for brief quotations in printed reviews, without the prior written permission of the author.

This is a work of fiction. All the characters in this book are fictitious, and any resemblßance to actual persons, living or dead, is purely coincidental. The names, incidents, dialogue, and opinions expressed are products of the author's imagination and are not to be construed as real.

Published by

köehlerbooks™

3705 Shore Drive
Virginia Beach, VA 23455
800-435-4811
www.koehlerbooks.com

Kip Langton

Victorian Stillness

a novel

VIRGINIA BEACH
CAPE CHARLES

The past is never dead. It's not even past.
—*William Faulkner*

PROLOGUE

ALL EXITS ARE FINAL. The man's trembling hand ran down the sleek gloss finish of the wenge wood banister, slipping past the black-and-white sign. A dream haze of neon light spray-painted the smoky-jazz air of the Café MigMag, and blue and red and green Christmas bulbs on the maraschino cherry-colored walls leaked into the art deco mirrors slanting downwards parallel to the stairs.

From the stairs these bulbs guided the unsteady hand to a bar that lived and breathed neon. It exhaled and inhaled through the LEDs underneath the glass holding the mountainous rows of liquor bottles, each its own source of luminescence with the glowing green and orange and brown piercing from the whiskey and the rum and the vodka. A beer sign hung on either side of this fireworks show of color. On one side, a neon yellow *Miller* with a neon blue *Genuine Draft* beckoned, and on the other, a red and blue bowtie-shaped Budweiser sign animated a lonely man smoking a cigarette at the bar. Above his drunken, drooped head, a TV hung from the ceiling. It played football. Giants vs. Saints.

"You wish to be seated?" a waiter in a tux asked.

"This game," the drunken man suddenly said to the waiter, clenching his arm. "You see this game. Atrocity. Like the universe."

"Yes, Mr. Orikal, like the universe."

"As the universe expands, dark energy—in the form of time and the speed of light—increases entropy and, consequently, flattens space and works against gravity until it no longer exists. The absence of gravity, matter, and the bending of space will create a paradoxical inevitability in both space and time, where a fully dematerialized universe made up of a hundred percent dark energy exists only at the speed of light, devoid of time, space, and any dimension. A dark energy universe will be infinitely infinitesimal and infinitesimally infinite. At this moment of full entropy, one hundred percent dark energy, which is infinite, and a hundred percent gravity, which is infinitesimal, will be one and the same. The dark energy-gravity paradox can only occur when there is no space, time, or dimension to dictate it and the instability of this absence will cause dark energy to immediately unhinge itself from its symmetry with gravity, causing another Big Bang event."

"That's right, Mr. Orikal," the waiter answered, gently and politely pulling the drunkard's hands off him.

The drunkard retreated to his seat as an ill-defined silhouette against the backdrop of atmospheric rainbow mud-splash and the bartender went on making drinks as sudden shades of blue lit her face like that blue-faced woman in Toulouse-Lautrec's *At the Moulin Rouge*. Illuminated, she turned on the rusted-over Bose speakers and Phil Spector's Christmas album played underneath the pulse of Café MigMag with fuzzy reverberations of the Ronettes classic "I Saw Mommy Kissing Santa Claus."

"You wish to be seated?" the waiter asked again.

"Yes," the man with the trembling hand answered.

"Please, right this way."

Startled by the drunkard, the man almost awoke from a dream to follow the waiter into Café MigMag's Rainbow Jazz Room. It was a storm of neon with the bulbs from the stairwell leading to nests of radiating color festooned on faux Fraser Firs. Round polished silver tables holding glowing white globes lined the walls where spectators sat stoically at their booths immersed in the watercolor of blue from *MIGMAG'S RAINBOW JAZZ ROOM* sign that enveloped the band playing steadily beneath it.

"Your table," the waiter said.

"Thank you," the man answered as he slid into the booth.

His hand continued to quiver, and he crossed his legs and then uncrossed them, unsure how to wait with calm and grace.

"What am I doing?" he asked himself.

The jazz band played on, and the black silhouetted spectators took no interest in his inner monologue of insecurities.

"Where is she?" he mumbled under his breath. "Always these places with her."

He closed his eyes to calm himself and leaned his stiff back against the booth. After a few minutes, he awoke as he heard her voice. "Always late. That's just who I am. Take it or leave it."

The waiter pulled out her chair.

"It's fine, Lez" he brushed off. "So . . .?"

"Well, guess that means let's get straight into it."

"Yes. Please. Into it."

"Got some land for you. I used to work there."

"Is that where—?"

"Yes, that's where it happened. And I know you'll want it."

PART ONE

American Standard

Many years earlier

"I think they're fine, Jeanne," Mr. Wood said.

"The one all the way to the right . . . ?" my grandmother asked.

"We'll see how it holds."

"Disease?"

"It's been after all the spruces."

My grandmother poured Mr. Wood coffee.

"Jeanne, did you do something different with this kitchen table?"

"You like the cloth?"

"Oh, yes. That's it. I do. I like the checkered pattern."

"Thought it was a nice change from bare wood."

"Yes. It is, Jeanne."

She sat at the table next to him.

"So," she said, "how's your leg?"

"Good."

"Good, as in . . . ?"

"Bad."

"Arnold!"

"It's o—"

"It's not okay, Arnold. We need to get that fixed."

"I went the other day. I'm just getting old. The leg is a little older than the rest of me."

"Please go to my guy."

"I like my guy."

"Please, Arnold."

"Okay."

"Let me call him up," my grandmother said.

She went into the den to make the call. Mr. Wood had his coffee and looked down at his leg.

"Are you around tomorrow, Arnold?" my grandmother's voice asked from the den.

"Tomorrow?"

"Yes."

"I think . . . yes, Jeanne, I am."

"Okay, can you please pen Arnold Wood in for Dr. Van Vactor at nine a.m. tomorrow," she told the nurse. "Nine a.m., Arnold . . . ?" she asked from the den. "Making sure . . ."

"Yes, Jeanne. Thank you."

She hung up the phone and walked back into the kitchen. "Now you can get that leg fixed." She sat back down next to him. "More coffee?" she asked.

"No, Jeanne, I'm fine."

"How's Fox?"

"Fox is good," he responded. "Fox Auto Repair is always good."

"Did wonders on my car. The brakes don't squeak. After all these years, the brakes don't squeak."

Mr. Wood laughed and poured himself more coffee. The second cup he would do himself.

"My son always said that Mrs. Scott always comes in with the easiest requests."

"I see the Frankenstein stuff he does around there. The way he takes apart things and manages to put them back together."

"He's always done that—my Fox."

"He has."

"Has he stopped by, Jeanne?"

"Not since the repair."

"I told him."

"Oh, Arnold, he doesn't have to stop by every week. He's a young man. With things to do."

"He should have manners and do what he should do. And I should do what I have to do and go out to pasture. *We're stuck between a generation that won't let go and a generation that won't hop on.*"

"Fox is one of the kindest men I know."

"Doesn't say much these days."

"Cut him some slack, Arnold."

"Jeanne Scott gives him a lot of business—and a lot of slack."

"I will continue to give him business and slack whether he comes to visit once a week or not."

"You're too kind."

"We're all family, Arnold. And Fox is a sweetheart, you know that."

Mr. Wood would now see me around the corner. I was shy with him, as I was with all older men.

"Osk," he said, "is that you there?"

"Yes," I responded. "Hi, Mr. Wood."

"How's it, Osk? Now Osk, how old are you now? Nine?"

"Eight," I responded in my shy way.

"You look like a nine-year-old, you know that. So, how's life for an eight-year-old, Osk? It's been a while for me."

I approached him with my arms against my side.

"Good," I answered. "Just playing."

"Playing what?"

"World War Two."

"Well," he said. "I played that game for real. Vietnam, I mean."

"I know, Mr. Wood. My grandmother said you were in Vietnam."

"Yes, I was."

"I wish I could play for real like you."

He laughed. He leaned back into his chair and finished his coffee.

"What happened to cowboys and Indians?" he asked my grandmother.

"Moved on, I guess," she answered.

"Well," he said, standing. "I better go. Now, Jeanne..."

"Yes...?" she fired back, sensing the momentum shift, readying herself for scrutiny.

"I can only say—"

"I know. I know."

"This property..."

"I know."

"It can't be everything."

"But it is."

"Yes, it is."

"Always will. See, I've been told success isn't about how much you want to win. It's about how much you're willing to lose. And I'm willing—oh God am I willing—I'm willing, Arnold, to lose everything for this."

"Jeanne, just don't lose yourself in it."

"I'm in it, Arnold."

"It's an old dream, this place. And it makes you become a memory of yourself if you stick to it too long. See, as I see it, the only way to get out is to live as a passenger in the disappointment of this present. To look back fondly at the long lost. To let nostalgia harden itself into that gravestone above us. This is what we do, Jeanne. We lay, finally, in that peace. We have to die to survive."

"You sound... Arnold, nowadays people here are getting awfully repetitive. You're sounding like the rest of them when you talk like this. You know that? What you sound like? And, worst, I'm sounding repetitive saying you sound repetitive."

"You know what I mean... what I'm trying to say..."

"It's not about me, Arnold. You know that as well as I do."

"I do, Jeanne. I sure as hell do."

She sighed as a distressed goodbye. "Nine a.m., Arnold."

"Yes, Jeanne, Nine a.m."

Later that night, I went out for a walk with my grandmother. We scanned along the stone wall, and I climbed and ran the stone wall while my grandmother made her way down the road. We stopped by a collapsed barn on the property, the trees bent inward and hunched over the wooden skeletal remains as if to protect or mourn the loss of that barn beneath them.

The wind picked up. It went in and out of the trees and pumped life into this landscape. The years gone by came back in with each Earth-driven breath. That melodic sway of youth receding underneath the church-arched ceiling of leaves. Only aging below. Only growing above.

"A storm," my grandmother said to me in front of the fallen barn.

I pointed in the direction it always came from.

"It's charcoal up there," I answered. I took that line right from my father. My grandmother laughed whenever I said that.

"Thunderheads," she said. "Gathering to give us a little fun tonight. We need it. The plants need it."

"Nature's chimes," I said, looking up at the leaves. "Mommy always said that about the leaves."

"She did."

"What do you think she's doing?"

"Well, it's hard to say."

"How?"

"Your mother. She was always on her own."

"I know that."

"She really was. Always. Out in the woods. Discovering. Just like you, Osk."

She pointed up at the leaves. "Listen," she said.

I listened and heard nothing.

"What?" I asked.

"Listen, Osk. Listen."

I listened harder and looked through the ever-shifting leaves into the sky. A kinetic and frenetic echoing turbine-tunnel scream churned itself into the storm. I could see some vantage point through a tunnel beyond the leaves pushed far behind me and the wind coming in from different directions and those flickering red lights ahead with wet-tire mist spitting out from traction and those mechanical sounds punching my ears and my hands clenching something right in front of me.

A clean exit.

From this tunnel.

Into a Vincent van Gogh starry sky.

The world danced all around me. "Crazy" by Patsy Cline played.

Then, I heard a voice.

Then, a drop of a spoon.

"Oscar," that voice said. "Baby, come on ... eat. Open that mouth of yours. Eat, baby. Eat."

"You hear it now?" my grandmother asked.

"Yeah. I can."

"So much of everything is up there," she said.

I could look without words like kids do when a moment in time surpasses their current wisdom.

"Everything," she said. "Your mother, your father ... your future. It's all up there. If you just listen. It's up there. Telling you. Whispering to you."

That drop of the spoon.

Cataclysmic.

The painted nose cone decompressing and flattening into some type of crushed papier-mâché against me, the pressure hurling me into an airborne tumbling frenzy through the shuddering and shifting tree leaves into the sky.

Then back down through the leaves.

That drop of the spoon.
Coming back to Earth.
Through the leaves.
That drop of the spoon, once again.
Coming back to Earth.
Through the leaves.
Once again.
Now motionless.
Heat building.
The world collapsing around me.
Footsteps approached.
A white cloud. In heaven, I assumed.
Those leaves dancing with the current of the clouds.
"Don't slip away, Oscar," a voice said. "Please, baby, don't leave me."
A spotlight bleeding through the canopy of the leaves.
A propeller strobing the light.
Wind caressing me.
One sweep across my face.
Another sweep across my face.
That light through the vibrating leaves.
And I was below.
Trapped.
Hidden.
Away with my grandmother on her property.
Next to this fallen barn.
Awaiting a storm. Those thunderheads congregating into one collective energy.

"Osk," my grandmother said, walking down the road back to the house. "We must go. The storm is here. Come on. We must go now."

I stopped looking up at the things to come and I ran along the stone wall to my grandmother. We went back to the house until the storm was over, dematerializing into that house.

Protected.

Safe.

Away.

In that house, Geneva had made a blueberry pie. It was a surprise. And, in that kitchen, she was waiting for us. Geneva sounded different to me because I was self-conscious about her place on my grandmother's property. My mind turned this proud, hardworking woman into a clownish relic of an age long gone. She really didn't sound like this. But it was how I imagined she sounded to others. Those who judged the hierarchy and lived by the standards of a modern society. This was the way they'd hear her. Beaten by White dominance. I would try not to hear it this way, but the self-consciousness would always take over. To an overly complex modern mind, when you saw a Black maid working for a White landowner, this is how you'd perceive it from your continual moral conditioning. And I wondered if I perceived everyone up here this way, with this false ear of mine. Maybe they were all cartoon sketches to me. But I couldn't help it. I would try to fight the conditioning. To comprehend things the way they were. For brief moments, I could hear the beauty of this true hidden reality. But then it would go away. There was just so much judgment out there. And the judgment twisted up into some screwed-up upside-down barometer measuring a self-inflicted, unstoppable pressure. God help me. I was a White straight male with property and my grandmother was an old White woman with servants, in the best sense of the word. There was a reason why I was quiet. I was embarrassed by all of it. And I felt I was boring being White and straight and fortunate. Blah blah blah. People like me had a voice for so long. Too long. My reign was over. Justly. Now I would shut up. Because no one wanted to hear me. Not anymore. I was pushed aside. Off in the dark somewhere. Backstage. The spotlight would now shed its illuminating self-importance on something new, something more interesting, something so freakishly distressed and modified by a burning hate that could be felt miles away. It was radioactive. This wasn't my time. But I was so young. What a shame. What a waste of youth. My time had passed before it had begun. And I couldn't even manage to play the underdog now. Couldn't manage to gather an ounce of attention. Because the past wouldn't allow me to. I was labeled the tyrant while my rights as a human being were suppressed by the new lawmakers of a stringent modern moral code. It was direct-injected anger. And anger like this could be as much a part of bad as it could be good. That was the scary thing. You could do so much bad in the name of good. And it scared me to the point I would shut up and be quiet about all of it. I would just think in the abyss and feel bad about the things I thought of. If only Geneva knew what she sounded like to me. How hurt she would be. Not because I heard her that way. But because I allowed the judgment to fracture my reality into mismatched pieces of self-reflective glass put back together by the people who hated everything this country stood for. That's the thing that would kill her. She had fought to be who she was, and the world was taking that away from her. It was trying to save someone who had already been saved. And the only way you can save someone who's already been saved is to strip them of their prized self-identified identity. You must bring them back to the battlefield. You must never let them forget what *we had done*. It's time to powerwash the muck that is the American Dream. That dream means nothing in the modern world. Because it can't be recycled into a controlled collective ideal. It's something selfless for the individual and only the individual. And it is found within us, unprompted and directionless, governed only by the thing that drives us, makes us who we always wanted to be—the dream of becoming. The America in us.

But not now. Now, it is the dream of being given. Waiting for a gift like a child does on Christmas. Did Santa come? And when this child finds no presents under his tree, he wants annihilation for not only himself but everyone else around him. We are the first generation in human history desiring its own extinction. Not because we hate ourselves but because we love ourselves so much more. We can't imagine time going on beyond our existence. We can't understand that the past wasn't there to lead to us and then end at us. No, it goes on. Into that ever-expanding unknown. That thing called the future. To not know you're just a building block to something far greater is to lose total connection with God. You become the devil of your own self-contained universe spun up by that red-hot tape of moral code and relevance.

"I be makin' ya something," Geneva said. "Yo favorite pie."

"Oh, Geneva, you didn't have to do that."

"When a storm is a-comin', we have them pies for Mrs. Jeanne and Mr. Oscar."

"Thank you," I said and sat down at the table.

"Gone on down by the barn?" she asked my grandmother.

"We did."

"You always gone on down by the barn, even when the weather is tellin' ya not to."

"Grandma doesn't care about the storm," I said.

"She bravin' it?"

"My grandma doesn't let it bother her. She is brave."

Geneva laughed. "I say not much bother Mrs. Jeanne."

"Can I have some pie?" I asked.

"Oh Lordeeee. Of course, y'gonna get some pie."

She cut a piece of pie and put it on my plate. It was the best—her blueberry pie.

"Geneva," my grandmother said, "there's nothing like your pies."

"Been makin' dem for centuries, Mrs. Jeanne. Naw, how's Mr. Wood holdin' up?"

"Oh, Geneva, he's getting old."

"Mr. Wood been getting' old for a looonnnggg time now."

"He's going to my doctor in the morning—finally."

"Ah, that's nice."

"The work is getting to him."

"It gets to us all, Mrs. Jeanne."

"That it does, Geneva. That it does."

I finished my pie and Geneva served me another piece.

"Mr. Oscar can finish a pie, can't he."

I felt bloated but remained silent.

Geneva laughed. "All pies. Mr. Oscar eatin' all types—apple, blueberry . . . that raspberry. Pie, and more pies."

The storm was over us.

"Sounds like we're in the middle of a racetrack," my grandmother said. "That wind is vicious."

The wind whipped through the screened-in porch and by the windows. It rolled over the house and came down the other side and bent the trees in the boundless woods. The sky was sitting low and the wall above us kissed the tips of a few of the trees.

"Did we shut the pool houses?" my grandmother asked Geneva.

"Bin shut all day, Mrs. Jeanne."

"How about the garage?"

"Shut."

"Thank you. You know how I get with these storms."

"Rathaa safe than sorry."

I finished my second piece of pie. Geneva and my grandmother didn't take notice. They looked out the windows.

"There goes one of our umbrellas," my grandmother said. The umbrella blew out of the hole in the center of the terrace table and flew across the lawn, hitting the stone wall. The metal pole of the umbrella got locked into one of the crevices of the stone wall and then remained still. My grandmother worried about it going onto the road, but she didn't have to worry now.

"Geneva," she said, "we'll have to repaint those tables."

"Ahh, yes."

"And you just painted them."

"More worse can happen, Mrs. Jeanne. Tornados."

"Oh, Geneva, please don't say that."

"Sorry, Mrs. Jeanne. You know wut I mean."
"It's been a while."
"Thank you, ole Lord."
"We've had tornados?" I asked with pie on my face.
"Years ago, Osk. Before you."
"What is a tornado like?"
"Like a freight train."
"A train . . . ?"
"Osk, it sounds like a train."
"Coming through the house?"
"Yes. We go down to the basement for that."
"How long?"
"Until it passes."
"Is the house all right after?"
"It depends."
"On what?"
"How strong it is. It destroys many homes. People lose everything."
I thought on this and wiped my mouth.
"Where do they go?"
"Some have no places to go."
"So, they just go nowhere?"

The wind grew in strength and the awnings clapped around and the flowerpots tipped over.

"My flowers," my grandmother said, dropping her head into her chest.

"Mrs. Jeanne, there's always more flowers to be had."
"You're right, Geneva. But those flowers."
"Better flowers than us."
"You're so positive. You've always been positive."

Geneva grew up in Charlotte, North Carolina. She came from a poor Black family, and she didn't talk about her past. This house was her new home and sometimes a cousin would come up to visit her. They were always very nice, each cousin, different each time. She had so many of them. My family wasn't big in comparison and Geneva always told my grandmother she hoped I would have a big family like hers one day. I would think about having a family. From the perspective of someone my age, family life was perpetual laughter and fun, devoid of loss and hardship. You thought that way as a kid. Because, why not?

"Mrs. Jeanne," Geneva said, pointing out the window. "You see that?"

My grandmother jumped from one window to the next, looking out in a panic.

"Yes, I do. What is that?"

"Ize got no idea."

A spotlight scanned along the windows from above somewhere and I could hear voices.

"Grandma?" I asked. "Do you hear that?"

"Are people in the woods, Geneva?"

"Beats me, Mrs. Jeanne. I hear dem."

"Oscar," I heard. "Baby, please. Eat, baby, please."

A spoon hit the ground.

"Something drop?" my grandmother asked us.

"Mrs. Jeanne, I hear that. Let me check in the pantry."

"Sounded like silverware falling or something like that."

"It do, Mrs. Jeanne."

Geneva hobbled into the pantry, and you could hear her looking through the cabinets. The voices became more audible from the woods.

"Why would people be out in the woods during a storm like this?" my grandmother asked herself. "It makes no sense."

"Mrs. Jeanne, there be some crazy people out there."

"Maybe it's the coyotes . . . ?"

"Maybe—dem coyotes sounds like that sometimes."

"I'm sure that's it. That would explain it. I'm sure they're running along the stream. Probably some poor fawn they caught."

"Mrs. Jeanne, don't say that."

"With the number of deer now, it wouldn't surprise me."

Geneva hobbled to her bedroom right off the kitchen and sat down on the edge of her bed.

"Everything all right, Geneva?" my grandmother asked.

"Oh, yes. All right. Tired is all."

"Take it easy."

"In this storm . . .?"

"Shut the door and take it easy."

"No dinner?"

"We'll figure it out."

"Mrs. Jeanne . . ."

"Please, Geneva, get some rest."

She shut the door, and you could hear the bed creak.

"Osk," my grandmother said to me, "she's having trouble."

"What trouble?" I asked.

"Her health and her family. I think she's going to go back to Charlotte for a little while."

"How long?"

"I don't know. There's something going on down there."

A crack of thunder.

"Yikes," I screamed.

I could hear crying from the woods.

"Is that crying?" I asked my grandmother.

"It's strange, isn't it. Well, we won't be going out there to check—not in this weather."

"Oh, God," a voice screamed. "No!"

"Grandma, are they all right?"

"I have no idea, Osk. But we're not going out there to check."

Geneva's TV went on and one of her favorite hospital soap operas played.

"I'm clear," a character said.

"You're clear," he said again.

"We're all clear," he said once again.

A crack of thunder. The windows lit up.

"I think it's time for the storm shutters," my grandmother said.

I ran upstairs and opened the windows to pull the storm shutter shut. My grandmother did this on the ground floor. Geneva had already done it from her room. The power then went out after a branch hit the wire that went from the house to the garage. With the storm shutters shut, my grandmother had to light a candle and you could see the flickering lightning penetrate through the edges of the shutters. The voices went away and there was a calm and the TV was off. Geneva was too tired to come out and fell asleep until morning. She normally didn't sleep well in silence. It was different tonight.

The next morning was bright and clear. Geneva was still asleep, and my grandmother fed the cats and let the dog out. I went out with the dog, Ernie, and jumped into the pond by the bottom of the hill on which the cottage stood. The cottage had one panoramic window that looked beyond this pond into our neighbor's property. They had a horse farm, and you would see the horses so still with their tails flapping around. I always wanted to go over there but never did. My grandmother had gone horseback riding there when my mother was young but hadn't gone since. I think my mother had been a very good rider. I think.

"Osk!" my grandmother called from the house. "Breakfast. Come up for breakfast. Make sure Ernie is dry."

"Yes," I yelled back. "I'm wet too."

"You both get dry then, you hear."

"Yes, Grandma."

We ran up the hill past the cottage and opened the wooden gate that connected to the stone wall. The gate had moss all over it and it always came off on your hands. I wiped my hands on my pants and grabbed a towel from the pool house. It took a while for Ernie to dry, and I finally came in for breakfast.

"That's why we don't have the dog go in so early," my grandmother said. "And you're still drenched."

It's hard for a boy to dry off when he also needs to worry about drying off the dog.

"Sit," my grandmother said.

I sat and had breakfast. Geneva was still asleep, and my grandmother didn't seem concerned. That meant she knew something I didn't know.

"Is Geneva fine?" I asked, chewing on the bacon.

"Tired today. But fine."

"I've never seen her sleep so long."

"I spoke to her before you woke up."

"She was up?"

"Yes. Back to sleep now. She's leaving later this afternoon for the city."

"Why would she do that?"

"You should ask her if you want to know."

"I don't want to."

"That's the way adults do it—they ask direct. That's how you become an honest man."

"I'm not a man."

"Not now. But soon."

"We'll see."

My grandmother laughed. "We'll see," she repeated to herself and went upstairs.

I was alone now, and Ernie started to sniff around. Not a sound came from Geneva's room and the door remained shut. That door was so still. Everything around Geneva had energy. She made you happy. And this door had no energy and no happiness.

"Hello," I heard from the front door.

I ran to the front and saw Mr. Wood through the screen door.

"Hey there," he said. "Is your grandma around?"

"She's upstairs. I can get her."

I ran up the stairs and tripped on the steps as I always did when I ran up to get my grandmother for visitors. She was always upstairs when visitors arrived. It was almost like she knew.

"Grandma," I said, now in her room. She was reading a book.

"Yes, Osk."

"Mr. Wood."

"Oh, he's back."

"Yes."

"Coming down. Take him to the kitchen."

I ran back down the stairs and opened the screen door.

"She's coming down," I said. "She wants me to bring you to the kitchen."

Mr. Wood smiled, took off his hat, and followed me to the kitchen. He was always so big in this small house. But that's how it always felt when men entered the farmhouse.

"Coffee?" I asked as he sat and placed his hat on the table.

"Yes. Thank you."

I poured him a cup that was way too full. He looked at it and then asked for a bottle of milk.

"Oh, yes," I said, scrambling to the pantry.

"Thank you," he said. By the time I got back with the milk, he had sipped the excess coffee away to make room for the milk.

"Sorry," I said.

He smiled and poured the milk in his coffee. Then we heard footsteps making their way down the stairs.

"Arnold," she called.

Mr. Wood stood up with the coffee in his hand.

"Jeanne, I have to thank you."

My grandmother entered the kitchen and made him a plate of bacon.

"Don't you dare," she said. "We all deserve some good medical guidance. Nothing more American than that."

"He looked at the leg and said I should really take it easy on it."

"No surprise there."

"I've just been too damn hard on it."

"No surprise there either."

"I'm going to have my nephew come by to help me out from now on. I can't do it all on my own anymore. It was a little selfish of me. Because I love this land. I want to do it all on my own. When I was a kid—"

"I know. I know. Arnold, you don't have to come here just to work. You know—"

"Yes. You tell me this."

"I mean it. It isn't all about work."

"What else am I going to do if I don't work?"

"You're always welcome to come here and visit me for a cup of coffee and some bacon."

Mr. Wood scratched his head and took a big slurping sip of the coffee. He was always a quiet sipper, so this surprised me.

"My nephew will do good work," he said in between sips. "He will."

"I'm sure he will, Arnold. You understand I will still pay you."

"Jeanne—"

"No, Arnold."

"That's not—"

"Absolutely," she said and pointed out the window. "Look out there. This is all you. You've always been there. No matter what happens, you've always been there."

Mr. Wood's hands began to tremble, and he began to cry.

"This damn leg," he mumbled.

My grandmother sat next to him and smiled. "Once you get to my age, it's 'this damn leg, this damn arm, this damn foot, this other damn leg . . . this damn everything.' You have it pretty darn good, Arnold. You need a break."

"I'm afraid of that," he confessed. "My nephew will do a good job. He knows this place. He's young. And he knows what he's doing. I promise."

"You don't have to promise a thing."

"I owe this land."

"We all do."

Mr. Wood stood and collected himself. He held his hat to his chest and finished his coffee. Thanking my grandmother, he limped through the house to the front door. My grandmother watched him from the kitchen and blew him a kiss.

"I'll have Eric come first thing next week," he said from the front porch.

"Looking forward to it. Eric's a good boy. Take care of yourself, Arnold."

"I feel like I'm in *Gone with the Wind*," she said to herself. "An end of an era."

I didn't respond because I didn't know what that was. My grandmother knew that, so that's why she said it to herself. She wasn't very good at explaining things sometimes, so I assumed I would learn it later in life somehow. For a kid, there's a lot of that "later in life" stuff.

"Osk," she said, bringing herself back to reality, "it smells like wet dog all over the place."

"I dried him."

"You sure about that?"

"I did."

"The smell doesn't indicate that, Osk."

"I don't know how much longer I could've dried him."

"Maybe a second more than the second you took to dry him."

I giggled, and she ran her hand through my hair.

"Poor Mr. Wood," she said to me. "Be thankful you're young. It can be very hard getting old."

The door blocking off Geneva's room was no longer silent. "He

Stopped Loving Her Today" by George Jones played. I could hear Geneva singing along to it. That was her favorite song. And that door didn't feel as sad as it had been. Then the knob turned.

"Geneva!" my grandmother yelled.

"Hi, Mrs. Jeanne."

"All is well?"

"As well as it can be."

"Bacon? Coffee?"

"I get to that, Mrs. Jeanne."

She hobbled to the coffee machine.

"Some fine coffee in the mornin'," she said, pouring herself a cup. "Fine, fine coffee."

"It's the good stuff, Geneva. Viennese roast. Pure heirloom typica. Arusha and mondo novo arabica—strictly hard bean." My grandmother read this off the bag of beans. She would make fun of things like this.

"Oh Lawd. Very rich. Apricots. Berries. Nuts. Sweat. And clean. Hmmm. Chocolatey."

Unlike my grandmother, Geneva tasted these notes. She wasn't kidding.

"Wish I had tastebuds like you, Geneva."

"Mrs. Jeanne, years of trainin'. Years and years and years."

"How are we this morning?"

My grandmother insisted Geneva sit at the table before she could make herself a plate of bacon.

"Mrs. Jeanne, I can get to that myself. Please, Mrs. Jeanne."

"No, no—you sit."

"Please, Mrs. Jeanne."

"Sit."

Geneva sat at the table and my grandmother put the bacon on the plate and served her.

"Today's the day," Geneva said.

"Everyone has family matters, you know."

"Lawd, I agree to dat more dan you know."

I noticed Geneva's accent grow when she thought about home. The music still played from her room and my grandmother began to sing along to it.

"I love this song," my grandmother said, swaying her hips.

"George Jones," Geneva cried. "George Jones."

"How about Dylan's 'A Hard Rain's A-Gonna Fall'?"

"That's your favorite, Mrs. Jeanne."

"It is."

"I be all George Jones. Got the jones for Jones."

My grandmother laughed and so did Geneva. I watched and smiled because I didn't get it. Kids could really smile at anything even if the thing they're smiling at goes over their head by about twenty-thousand feet.

The song ended and my grandmother spotted something out the window.

"Hear that?" she asked us.

I hopped out of my seat and darted to the window to see.

"What?" I asked.

Geneva remained seated and said she didn't hear anything.

"Is someone playing George Jones out there . . . ?"

"Mrs. Jeanne, you be all right?"

"No. Seriously. I hear your song, Geneva. Out there, in the woods. I swear."

I listened hard. The melody revealed itself suddenly. Then it went away. Then it came back in waves.

"Those voices," my grandmother said, slamming her ears against the glass. "What in the name. Who's out there?"

"Gosh, Mrs. Jeanne. I do hear that. It makes no sense. Playing the same song. Is someone prankin' us?"

"I don't know, Geneva. This is very weird."

"Odder than odd, Mrs. Jeanne."

"What in the name."

"Call the cops."

"Wait. Let me go out."

"I wouldn't."

"Give me a second."

She opened the back door, and I watched her follow the sound into the woods.

"No one messes with Mrs. Jeanne," Geneva said to me.

I continued to watch my grandmother and nod my head to Geneva's comment of reassurances. I wasn't someone who needed to be reassured when I was distracted with anticipation and possible doom. Even if it was my grandmother, I hate to say.

We waited for her to come out. Time went slower, as it always did. No appearance yet. Tick. Tock. Tick. Tock. No appearance yet. And then that music came in a swell. There was the voice of George Jones singing again.

Then a voice said, "Baby, you gotta eat. He has to eat—baby, eat."

"Oscar," another voice called.

I jumped up and down. "Geneva," I yelled. "They're calling me!"

"Don't you be getting out, too."

"But Geneva!"

"No, Mr. Oscar. Wait for Mrs. Jeanne comin' back."

"Mitch, I can't anymore," it said.

I opened the window and called out to the voice in the woods.

"I'm here," I yelled. "I'm here. I'm here. I'm here."

Geneva pulled herself off the seat and grabbed me.

"Enough, Mr. Oscar."

She shut the window and sat back down, tired from her burst of energy.

"Can I . . . ?" I asked, sitting next to her.

"You can look out—datz all."

"Promise."

Back at the window, I saw my grandmother returning from the woods to the house. Her hands were in the air to signal she found no one.

"Oh my God!" the voice said. "Look! Look! Oh my God, Mitch!"

"Oscar," the other voice said.

Ignoring Geneva, I opened the window again and called out: "I'm here. Oscar—that's me. I'm here. In the house. Where are you calling me from? I'm here. You're so close. I'm here. I'm here. I'm here. In the house."

My grandmother's walk turned into a fast jog. I had never seen her run like that. It scared me. She was running right toward me. And she had her finger against her mouth to quiet me down as she ran right to my window.

I dropped to the ground and knelt below the window, crying because she had really scared me. To have the one person you trusted most in the world terrify you like that is something almost impossible to describe, especially for a kid like me. It made the world collapse on itself. And it did. In a state of panic, I passed out, unsure I ever wanted to see my grandmother again.

Blackness.

My eyes shifted around a blank space.

No up.

No down.

A barren . . .

Motionless . . .

Ocean.

Of.

Nothingness.

"I can see his eyes moving," someone said. "See his eyes?"

"We've seen this before. Come on. Come outside. Let's get out."

"Look!"

The nothingness opened into hints of gray that faded off into a bright white. Like linen over my eyes, I could now see images without the defining features. The silhouettes moved about, and one pulled the other toward it. They became one object.

"Stop," it cried.

The object split and the linen was pulled from my eyes, and everything became pink and yellow and then straight to that blackness within the recesses of my mind.

"I love you," it said. "I'll always love you. Come back to me, baby."

A pull like I had never felt before. A force beyond that of Earth. My being sucked straight out of my mind and out into a room where I lay. A woman over me, crying and hugging me. Then that gravity of life came back. That pull. But back into my body. Back into my mind.

I could hear nothing.

Feel nothing.

Then, a sparkle.

Growing and shrinking.

Ignited.

Extinguished.

At the end of the endless.

Way away.

Now, a glowing object coming closer.

Running toward me.

And a voice calling me from somewhere else. "Come back, baby," it repeated.

My eyes stayed on this moving object.

Closer and closer and closer it got.

"Osk," this object yelled. "Stay away from the voice."

I turned to flee from it. But it was too fast. I turned back to look at it. I could see it was my grandmother, lit like a Christmas tree. A human star. I tried to jump out of the way, and she put her finger to her mouth to hush me as she closed in on me.

"Stay away from the voice," she screamed right before her flaming body intercepted mine. "Stay out of the damn woods! Out of the woods! Out of the woods! Out of the woods!"

Hot, piercing light all around me. I was wrapped within my grandmother, and I spun in the air. The ground and the sky circled around me and blended into one milkshake of luminosity. I was flipping in the air, the ground stopping me and throwing me back up. My grandmother held me. She kept me inside whatever it was I was in. Tumbling. And tumbling. And tumbling. All the while, "He Stopped Loving Her Today" played from somewhere within that vibrant hue. It was clear—the longing in George Jones' voice. And in that hue, I could see the silhouettes again and I heard one of them crying again.

"This was his favorite song," it said.

"He can't hear it," the other said.

The other silhouette walked away, and I was left with the crying one. She sang along to the song. I tried to sing along with her. But nothing. No air to fuel the words. Total vacuum.

"What got into you, Osk?" my grandmother asked as I came to. I was flat on the floor and Geneva placed a wet, cold rag on my forehead. She then rolled it up into a ball and dabbed my face.

"My sweet chile," she said. "You got all up in worry."

I sat up on the ground and rubbed my eyes.

"Not too fast," Geneva said, holding me up. She sat with me on the ground and my grandmother watched me from above.

"Osk, you fine?" she asked.

I wouldn't respond in my confusion.

"Well, you seem fine now," she answered herself.

"I saw . . . I saw—you coming . . . from the woods," I stumbled to say.

"Then I saw you drop, Osk. Straight to the ground when I came in."

"You were running."

"Running?"

She looked over at Geneva and laughed.

"Yes."

"I haven't run in a decade, at least."

"You weren't running . . . ?"

My grandmother uneasily knelt on the floor and placed the back of her hand against my forehead.

"You don't seem to be burning up," she said.

"Grandma, I'm worried."

She gave me a hug and told me not to worry. This had never happened to me before, and I thought I was losing my mind.

"Am I losing it?" I asked.

My grandmother stood and let Geneva handle the question.

"Chile, ya too young to be losin' it."

"So, later on I will?"

They both laughed.

"Do I seem crazy, Osk?" my grandmother asked from the pantry.

"No."

"Does Geneva seem crazy?"

"No."

"Then the odds are in your favor."

"I guess craziness is passed down," I said, more to myself. But they overheard and they both laughed.

"Ize a-gree with dat," Geneva said. "Crazzzy go to one another."

"Up, up," my grandmother said, coming from the pantry with a loaf of bread in her hands. "Can't sit on the floor all day."

She pulled me up from under my arms and I balanced on my rubber legs. Geneva made sure I didn't fall.

"All good?" my grandmother asked me.

"Yes."

"Good."

"Mr. Oscar won't be goin' in datz liquor cabinet no more."

I didn't get the joke and rubbed my eyes out of embarrassment. My grandmother laughed for me.

"Geneva," she suddenly said, "you gotta get going."

"Ahhh yes. Ize be gettin."

"Wait, it's still early, right? My timing is off today."

"Nahhh, with my speed, Ize be gettin."

Getting on a plane was a big deal for people in my family. You overprepared and got there early. The departure from this plot of land felt like a departure from Earth straight to the moon. And it was a little airport we went to. About ten miles away. It touched the edge of our property line. At night, we could always see the planes take off over the pool, their blinking lights full of wonder as they broke through the clouds, the relay of sound from the engines soon stretching to the point of inaudibility. Far off they would go, outside this little snow globe of acreage we had to ourselves.

And when Geneva left to head to that airport, I sat by the pool with my grandmother, and we waited there until her time of departure and we saw her plane take off and we waved to her, assuming she was waving back at us from one of those little windows. I was curious about what her life was like in Charlotte. Was she the same there? I would never get to know. Then that got me thinking about what she was like alone. Did she even wave to us from the plane? Did she even like us as much as it seemed? Questions a kid would ask only to himself. Because my grandmother would have said, "Osk, of course she is!"

◆

About a week later, I came down to the kitchen to find my grandmother crying. She wouldn't look up at me and kept her hands against her eyes and mouth. It looked like she was suffocating herself and her heaving breathing came through the openings between her fingers. All I could do was watch. She knew I was there.

"Everything is where it always is," she said to me.

I got up and served myself. The bacon wasn't fully cooked, so I put it back on the pan for a few minutes. My grandmother never let me cook for myself and she didn't seem to care. Something was very off. Now I wasn't just in awe; I was scared and concerned. The transition from awe to fear for a child takes longer than it does for adults. It did for me, at least.

"What's wrong?" I finally asked, sitting at the table with my fully cooked bacon.

After a few tries, she answered: "Poor Mr. Wood."

"What happened to Mr. Wood?"

"He died, honey."

I wouldn't cry but rather blinked rapidly from the surprise.

"I'm so sorry, honey," she said, and revealed her red-and-white-blotched face. You could see the finger lines in her fair Irish skin. She didn't look like herself and it spooked me.

"It was sudden," she continued. "Very sudden." She fell into her hands again and cried, "Oh, Arnold!"

Later in life I found out how Mr. Wood died. My grandmother told me by accident because she had forgotten she hadn't told me. That was a strange way of finding something like this out. It was always a heart thing in my mind. You always assumed it was a heart thing with hardworking men in this area. Never what it really was for sure. Suicide was not a possibility. People were happy there. And Mr. Wood was happy and loved his family and loved the land. He was found dead in a Beer World with his wrists cut open. "Went up the wrists vertical—didn't want to be saved," as my grandmother put it later. And I remember that Beer World bathroom. Things like that I always remembered. That water-stained framed poster above the American Standard toilet. It was a Grandmaster Flash and the Furious Five poster.

But that day, I had no idea. So, it stayed as a heart thing. My grandmother relied on my innocence to protect me from the truth.

"He should've never gone to my doctor," she moaned and sniffled. "He never wanted to go. I should've left it alone. I took the oxygen out of everything he did by doing that to him. He wasn't that type of man. And I ruined him."

I couldn't understand how you could ruin someone by taking them to the doctor. I thought the doctor helped. They helped me. And they helped my grandmother. But I guessed, at the time, they hurt some people. And the days went fast into nights after we found out Mr. Wood had died.

At night, my grandmother would make my dinner in total silence, and I would look out the window at the woods and see that definitive tree line dividing the blackened gray sky from the blackened green crowd of trees below it. The woods looked like a wall all around us and the clouds roamed over this wall to peek inside this sheltered place my grandmother had protected for so many years. Soon to be passed down to me, she told me. And she said it again that night when I was looking out the window at the woods. She broke her silence.

"That will be all yours," she said. "And then you'll pass it down to your kids. And then they'll pass it down to their kids. And so on . . . generations to come . . ."

"What if I don't have kids?" I asked.

"You wouldn't want kids?"

"I don't know."

"Who wouldn't want to have kids?" she asked.

"I am a kid."

"When you're not a kid."

"I have to have a wife—have a mom . . . for the kids."

"Yes, you would."

"I don't know."

"You're not supposed to."

I couldn't take my eyes off those woods.

"You're always staring out there, Osk."

"It's dark."

"Mysterious dark? Or scary dark?"

"I don't know."

"Osk, you're full of 'I don't know's."

"Yeah."

"Tell me."

"I guess . . . scary."

"Why would you look at it then?"

"I guess . . . because we never go."

"So, it's also mysterious."

"Yeah."

"The airport is right there; it can't be that mysterious."

"I guess not."

"It is dark," she said. "That's for sure."

"Grandma, is Geneva coming back soon?"

"Few days."

"She's been gone a while."

"She has."

"Why?"

"You know. Family problems."

"Yeah. Yes."

She plopped the mashed potatoes on my plate and put the sliced steak on top of it. My favorite were the peas. They were always in a separate bowl, but I drizzled them on top after my grandmother poured up the chocolate milk. It was a heavy meal. But that's what Geneva did. And my grandmother would follow her tradition.

"Eat up, Osk," she said and searched for something in the pantry. I could hear pots and pans moving around and a sudden crash of the thing she wanted against the floor.

"Ah," she said. "Here it is!"

Returning to the table, she watched me eat. She was excited about this steak. It came from her friend's local farm. I took a bite and felt self-conscious.

"Well . . ." she said.

"It's good, Grandma."

"How good?"

"Really good."

"See, I can never really tell with you. You're too polite. We made you too polite."

"I really like it."

"Hmm. Okay."

"I really do. Very . . ." I couldn't think of the word.

"Tender?"

"Yes."

"What does tender mean?" she asked.

"Soft."

"Hmmm. Okay."

"The grass is high," I commented, to get off the steak talk.

"Yeah—without Mr. Wood . . ."

"I can try."

She laughed. "You're not big enough for that machine."

"I can do it."

"No, you can't. Osk, I have doubts about that nephew."

"Which nephew?"

"Mr. Wood's."

"How come, Grandma?"

"It won't work. He hasn't been around. His word died with his uncle. We're gonna need some help around here. How would you feel about a couple I heard about from the city?"

I wondered why she was asking me. Why would I care about a couple coming from the city? I didn't ask. But I wondered about it—to myself, as always. I was quiet from the outside and loud in my mind. Guess that's why I'm writing this book . . .

"Osk?" she asked again.

"That's okay," I answered, like there was a reason for me to care and I decided to give it my blessing.

"Good. Good," she sighed.

"How do you know them, Grandma?" I asked.

"A friend of a friend—Silvia . . . you remember her, right?"

"Silvia . . . ?"

"Yes, she came up here a few times with her two boys. What were their names . . . ? Ah, yes, Ben and AJ."

"Oh yeah. I remember them. They were nice."

"Yes, nice boys."

"They liked the pool."

"They lived in that pool," my grandmother laughed, very stuck in the memory. "Anyway, Silvia knows this couple from the city who really want the country life. I don't think the experience is there, but the desire is. Osk, we kinda don't have a lot of options."

My grandmother did this a lot. She would talk to me like she was talking to herself. It was more therapy than real conversation. It helped her think things through. And I was happy to be the sounding board.

"Are they coming up?" I asked.

"Same day Geneva gets back. Timed it so she can meet them."

"Really?"

"Yup."

I got nervous when new people came up. I never knew what to say.

"Oh, come on, Osk," she said, sensing my anxiety. "They're nice people who really want to be here."

"So, they'll live here . . . ?"

"Yes, if we hire them."

"Where?"

"We'll build them a house. Well, it'll have to be a small prefabricated place—but it'll still be nice."

"Where?"

I followed her to the back door, and she pointed at the plot of land behind the garage.

"There," she said.

"Oh, that's a good spot, Grandma."

"It is, isn't it. Wish it didn't have to be a prefab house. Nothing that can be done about that, though. We just don't have the money anymore."

For a kid, asking questions was easy. But I was tapped out.

Geneva came back as her old self. Whatever it was she had to deal with in Charlotte was resolved and she had a freshness about her that made the whole property feel alive. "He Stopped Loving Her Today" played all throughout the house and Geneva would walk by me singing along with George Jones. I knew all the words by this point, but I never sang along. I was too embarrassed to. I was too embarrassed to do a lot of things. But I guess that's normal for kids. At least that's what I assumed at the time. I would always assume things about myself—a way of shrugging my shoulders and moving on.

"Geneva," my grandmother said, slapping Geneva in the butt, "you've got some pep in that step. You met a Mr. Geneva, or something like that?"

Geneva slapped my mother back. "Lawwwddd, I would."

"Geneva!"

"Whuttt—we all need a George Jones."

My grandmother almost fell to the floor laughing and Geneva hit her with a rag again to get her to stop laughing because it was making her laugh.

"Mrs. Jeanne," she mumbled. "Whennzzz . . ." Her words couldn't break through the laughter. "Mrs. Jeanne," she attempted again. "Ahhh, Gawwdd."

It was infectious and they both made each other worse. The Irish skin on my grandmother's face was tomato red.

"Well," my grandmother said, collecting herself. "We're very happy you're back."

"Thank yaaa, Mrs. Jeanne."

"Osk, too."

"Thank yaaa, Mr. Oscar."

I smiled and then looked down.

"So," Geneva went on, "Ize hurd we'll be havin' some guests—today."

"Yes," my grandmother answered, like she had never laughed before. "We are. From the city. We're thinking they could help out around here. Be good caretakers."

"Gettin' sum caretakers..."

"It's... it's getting... you know, Geneva. We need a lot more here now. Arnold was overwhelmed. He loved it. But he was overwhelmed. Everything... the weather is just crazy. The lawn is burnt. And I don't think you're hopping on that machine—"

"I say I would not, Mrs. Jeanne."

"Me neither. And a lot more than that. We need someone to manage the hay now for the ag breaks. Wally and Debby are moving down to Florida with the horses."

"Why?" Geneva asked.

"Horse shows. More of them down there than up here. And I don't want those fields to turn to woods. The loggers also want to come in. That time has come. I need someone, Geneva. I'm getting too old for all of this. We need the support. We need caretakers now. I'm usually the last one to admit things. But I'll be the first one to admit this. Wish we could do it all on our own. But we can't. We just can't."

"I hear, Mrs. Jeanne. I'm sure they're a fine caretaker."

The day went on, timeless, as it always did in this tiny universe of woods with a Victorian farmhouse in the middle of it. Not once did I ever check the time there. I would know by the light and how my grandmother acted, and the way Geneva reacted to my grandmother. Being the quiet one in the family, I felt I was the listener, the one who had his eyes above the snow globe looking into this little house. In a way, thinking like this made me feel significant. There was a reason for my silence. It elevated me, in my own mind. And a lot is in your own mind when you're a kid.

So, when the potential caretakers entered the property, I imagined I could see them from outside the snow globe looking in. I could see my eyes peering down into rounded, reflective glass. Like a hawk perched up somewhere, I watched that yellow car worm through the property, making its way to the house. There was something parasitic about it. The way that car moved. I saw them pull in and I spotted through the windshield a blue handicap placard dangling from the rearview mirror. Its reflective surface caught the sun and there was something so imposing in the way it caught those rays and knifed them into my eyes.

The doorbell then rang.

And rang again.

And then again . . . and again . . . and again.

"Holy mackerel," my grandmother said, "I'm coming. I'm coming."

She made her way from the back of the house to the front, and Geneva followed behind her. I waited in the back at the kitchen table. But I leaned over from the chair to see what was going on.

"Hello, hello!" my grandmother said, opening the screen door.

"Hyzzz," Geneva said.

The woman was tall and had wild hair escaping from the containment of her hat. The longer gray strands popped out of her head like twigs, and they absorbed the light, making her silhouette glow along its edges. Later in life, I would realize she looked exactly like Sally from Tim Burton's The Nightmare Before Christmas. That circular face. The pale skin. Those big round eyes. Even the daddy long-leg walk she had with her white-and-black T-shirt with the two C's interlocked over the word CHANEL loosely draped over her tight raw denim jeans with the word GUCCI spilling down the side of each ankle into her oversized gray and black Nike Jordan 1 shoes. On her head, she wore a jet-black Rag & Bone nylon baseball cap with a pair of Oliver Peoples sunglasses kissing its brim.

"Hi," this heavily branded woman said, removing her sunglasses and hat as a form of disarmament.

She towered over Geneva and my grandmother. And she seemed distressed by the bags she was carrying. Almost like it was my grandmother's fault she had those bags. At least that's what it felt like to me.

"May I . . . ?" the woman asked, already scooting her way through the narrow hallway.

"Of course. Of course," my grandmother answered. "Come to the kitchen."

"So pretty," the woman said. "We love farmhouses. The country, really. Anything country. It's cute. And small. Charm. Lots of charm."

She dropped her bags loudly on the kitchen floor and asked if she could sit. There was a lot of effort put into everything she did. Not effort to help. But effort to complain or make us feel bad about her present condition, whatever that was at the time. I could already tell she took a lot out of you by simply being there. My grandmother didn't seem to notice this. But I could tell Geneva was a little skeptical. She was very expressive, and it was easy to tell when she didn't like people. Her eyes had a questioning look, and I knew that could transition into dislike very fast.

"Lez, right?" my grandmother said. She crossed her legs and sat too close to the woman. The woman was alarmed by the lack of personal space given to her.

"Yes, Lez it is. Jeanne . . . ?"

"Yup. That's me. And this is Geneva. And this is Oscar. I call him Osk."

"Hey, Osk," she said, her dark eyes locked on me. Shark eyes.

"Hi," I said, looking down. It wasn't a good sign she went straight to the nickname without getting to know me first. That meant she assumed things too fast and didn't care enough to get to know me. Like people who buy things already worn so it looks like they created the patina even though they had it for less than twenty-four hours. I didn't trust people like that. And I didn't trust her.

"Hello, Geneva," she then said. Those shark eyes shifted over to Geneva and locked onto her.

"Nice to be meetin' ya," Geneva said in her unsure way.

"Where's your husband?" my grandmother asked, confused.

"Oh, he's coming. Lugging a lot of stuff."

"You're just coming for the day, aren't you?"

The woman, who I will now call Lez, was offended by the question. But she still answered in her icy hot way.

"We're staying at a little inn in Livingston Manor."

"Oh, that's wonderful. I hear Livingston Manor is really turning around."

"Yes. It is."

The man came through the back door like he had lived in this house for decades. Not even Mr. Wood came in through the back door. That was something you didn't do here.

"Oh, Rudge," Lez said, and stood. "Slaving away per usual. Let me help you."

She said that in a way that suggested we should help him. But we didn't. Because it wasn't our problem they came in with bags. Matter of fact, why would they even bring bags into the house if they weren't staying here? It made no sense. And I think my grandmother was too distracted to even think that far. Geneva was too displeased to think that far.

"Hi," the man said, shaking my grandmother's hand. "I'm Rudge."

Rudge looked like a fake lumberjack.

"Please, sit," my grandmother said, so intrigued by them. They had an aura I couldn't figure out. Maybe my grandmother had.

"Thank you," Rudge said.

"Why didn't you guys leave the bags in the car?" my grandmother thankfully asked about this very large elephant in the room.

Lez spoke before Rudge could.

"We don't like to leave things in the car," she answered. "If these bags were stolen, that would be it for us—done. Rudge would have to slave away more in that hot kitchen he worked in for years to get these things back. And his poor back. The way they treat him there."

◆

I could hear a steady beeping, setting the pace of "He Stopped Loving Her Today" by George Jones.

◆

My grandmother, being my grandmother, was genuinely concerned. She really did care for humanity. Even for people who didn't have her best interest at heart. It was her Christian mind. "The mind of America," she'd say.

"That's so awful," she said. "We wouldn't want you losing your things. I do have to say, though, it's very safe here. We never lock the doors. This house is as safe as can be."

"You don't lock the doors?" Lez asked.

"No, never. It hasn't been a problem."

"There was a home invasion in Liberty last week."

My grandmother was shocked. "What?" she asked.

"Just last week. They broke in and beat up the woman and took her guns. She was hospitalized."

"How . . ." my grandmother muttered and looked at me and Geneva. "How did we not hear about this?"

Geneva was startled and I was startled that Geneva was startled.

"Not a thing I hear," Geneva said.

"Her house was not as nice as this. And you guys are so isolated. You never know. God forbid if those criminals ever discovered this beautiful, secluded place. What would it take . . . twenty minutes for the cops to get here . . . ?"

"We don't know," my grandmother panicked. "Never thought of it."

"At least, I bet. These beautiful paintings you have here. Saw some of them in the hallway."

"Yes, those are my husband's."

"What a talent."

"Yes."

Rudge was as quiet as I was, and Geneva wouldn't sit. She never sat with people she didn't trust.

"Someone can come right in here and run off with them. Pack them into their truck and you'll never see your husband's paintings ever again. I'm guessing he passed?"

Lez said it like she felt his spiritual presence in the house. She reminded me of a witch, and I was frightened by her. I wondered if Rudge was, too.

"Eleven years ago," my grandmother sighed. "He was a wonderful painter. Didn't sell a painting, though. Only kept his art for the family. He was an architect. That's what paid the bills. But he did love it. Though, the passion was the art. Scotty is all over the walls now. It's his legacy on those walls."

"Jeanne," Lez cried. "His legacy can be gone—like that . . . gone!"

Geneva inhaled and was even more dissatisfied with these guests.

"Ize be needin' some air," Geneva announced.

"Oh, oh, yes, Geneva," my grandmother answered with that faraway voice, inundated by this new sense of total paranoia.

Geneva hobbled to the back door and had to kick it open because of the humidity. The door slammed shut and you could hear her legs dragging around outside. I could tell she was getting very tired. The whole place was getting very tired.

"That would be an awful thing," my grandmother said, stuck in Lez's trance.

"It would be."

Rudge had a look of admiration. His smirk was so subtle, but you could see some sort of sick and twisted arousal he got out of his wife's crafted manipulation. It felt like he had seen this many times before.

"Is she okay?" Lez asked my grandmother as her long neck retracted to get a better view of Geneva.

"Oh, yes . . . why?"

"She's been here a long time."

"Yes, she has."

"How long?"

"Oh, God. Over forty years."

"Isn't that something."

"It is. She's family."

"Where's her actual family?"

"Charlotte."

"Ahhh."

"She just came back from visiting them."

"Ahhh."

"What?"

"Trouble?"

"No."

"Oh."

"There's always family drama."

"There is," Lez smiled. "And there's always a breaking point."

"True."

"And she lives in that room?" Lez asked.

"Yes."

"Tiny room . . ."

"Really? It's the same size as the rooms upstairs."

"Seriously?"

"Of course. These are farmhouse rooms."

That comment annoyed Lez. You could tell she liked the idea of a farmhouse but didn't like the people who came with it.

"Can we see the rest of the house?" Lez asked and nodded at Rudge to get up. Rudge got up like a dog would. Quick, and thereafter, ready to take the next command. Good dog, Rudge.

My grandmother stood. "Right this way," she said.

Lez and Rudge followed behind my grandmother, and I followed behind them. The stairs creaked as we went up and Lez felt too hyper for this house. She always made faces when the wood made a sound, and it annoyed me. Even at my age, it annoyed me.

"This house is very vocal," my grandmother said, reaching the last step to the second floor.

"It's such a cute old house," Lez said. Rudge moved his head around to agree. He looked the most country here and you assumed he was ready to cut down a few trees. But he really was a dud. Lez was a high-functioning live grenade.

My grandmother showed her my room and the other guest rooms and what would be her room. The house was small but had a lot of rooms. Seven rooms in total. Geneva had one on the first floor. The second floor had four. And the third floor had two.

"Do you ever use all these rooms?" Lez asked. You had to be careful how you answered questions with Lez because she seemed like the kind of person who would take a mental note and use it against you later.

"It's rare," my grandmother answered. "When my mother was around, the house was filled up every weekend."

"I see."

"My mother saw this as more of a summer home. She would only come up on the weekends and stay in Westchester on the weekdays."

"I see."

"I went back to the tradition of living here year-round."

"Okay."

My grandmother was overexplaining herself and I didn't know why.

"There's a lot of moving parts to this place," my grandmother said.

"I bet—a property this size."

We finished looking through the second floor and went up to the third.

"We call this the boys' room," my grandmother said, turning on the lights. It was always very dark on the third floor.

"Very cute," Lez commented.

"And this, the girls' room."

"Cute. What a marvelous place you have here, Jeanne. Really marvelous."

"Thank you. We try."

We went back down, and Rudge missed a step and fell down the stairs. I had never seen someone fall in the house before, and I didn't know how to react. I laughed a little to myself because it looked so dramatic to see this lumberjack tumble down the stairs like that.

"Oh my God!" my grandmother screamed.

Lez helped Rudge up and my grandmother tried but she was too old to be effective. It was funny because Lez and Rudge acted way older than my grandmother. They never mentioned their age, but I guess around forty-five, maybe fifty.

"It's the hot kitchen," Lez said, holding Rudge. "They're working him to death in that hot kitchen."

I wondered what this kitchen was like. She kept mentioning it and I pictured it as the depths of hell. Poor Rudge, cooking for the devil.

"I'm fine," he finally said. He didn't want Lez to hold him anymore.

"You sure? You're just so overworked."

"Yes, Lez. I'm fine."

She let him go and watched him do it on his own like a mom letting go of the bicycle. And she remained right behind him without him knowing so she was there to catch him if he fell. They really had a way of making you feel guilty for not having such problems. Morality was built out of ailments for them. We were less fragile, and because of that, we were somehow the oppressors. I felt bad I wasn't the one who fell down the stairs.

When we returned to the kitchen, Lez had Rudge sit down at the table with both of his legs up on one of the chairs. She didn't ask my grandmother and pulled up a chair and placed a pillow under Rudge's feet from Geneva's room.

"They overwork you so," she repeated in a baby voice.

"I'm fine, please," Rudge insisted, now embarrassed.

"You always say you're fine and you're not. You think of other people too much. You need to start thinking of yourself."

"Please," he repeated.

"Osk," my grandmother said. "Would you be able to sit back with Rudge?"

I didn't want to be alone with him.

"Osk . . . ?"

"I can stay," Lez chimed in.

"No. No. Osk?"

I nodded my head.

"Good. If Rudge needs anything, please get it for him."

They went outside and I watched them through the window, ignoring Rudge while he ignored me. My grandmother showed Lez where she wanted to build their house. I hoped this wouldn't work out. I really didn't like them. But it always wound up working out with the people you didn't like. They had a way of making you feel like you needed them more than they needed you. In this case, Lez had the upper hand.

It was nearing an hour before they came back. They'd gone up the road and back down toward the cottage and the pond. My grandmother opened the back door and Lez agreed to take the first step into the house without hesitation. She seemed very competitive in the way she moved.

"How's my poor husband?" she asked Rudge in a baby voice.

"Better than ever," he responded, cringing to add to the drama. My grandmother felt bad this had happened in her house and Lez let my grandmother take the blame by continuing to ask how Rudge was.

"If only you could've gone on that walk," she said and then kissed Rudge. He accepted her kiss with a dumb look on his face. Like a goat or something accepting praise from its owner.

"I would've loved to," he answered.

"I'm so sorry, Rudge," my grandmother said.

Lez remained quiet and let her husband respond.

"No worries," he said.

"Those stairs can be a menace."

"Quite all right."

"Maybe," Lez interjected, "maybe you can put some yellow markers on the edge so people can see better. It would've surely saved my husband the pain."

"I never thought of that. I will surely do that."

"Those steps are dangerous," Lez said, somehow taken by her husband's face. "I love you, Rudge-Rudge," she continued, squeezing his cheeks.

"Osk," my grandmother asked, uncomfortable with the strange behavior. "Osk" was always her safety word for changing the conversation.

"Osk," she said again, "where's Geneva?"

"I haven't seen her," I answered.

"You haven't?"

"No."

"It's been an hour. You haven't seen her at all?"

"She hasn't come to the house."

"I hope she's all right."

"Should I look for her outside?"

"Yes."

That was my ticket out of there, far away from this bizarre couple. I kicked the door open and ran out screaming "Geneva!"

I couldn't find her anywhere and stayed away from the woods. I went to the pool and checked in the pool houses even though there was no reason for her to be there. Unless she was hiding. I wanted to hide too.

"Geneva!" I screamed.

I skipped down to the garage and went up the stairs to the apartment above. And there she was, sitting on the bed with the TV on.

"Hey," she said to me, opening her arms. I gave her a big hug. I acted like I hadn't seen her in months, and she acted like she hadn't seen me in months.

"Why are you here?" I asked.

"Ize watchin' dis horrible show."

"Why are you watching it if it's horrible?"

"I ain't findin' dis prayer network. Found this horrible thing instead. Listin' to it."

The old TV was pixelated and the man on the screen was dressed like he was on the Starship Enterprise.

"I urge you," he almost sang, "to put aside the childish fantasy of religion. Think critically."

He grasped at something in the air and pulled this invisible object to his chest. Parts of his body were cut off from the pixelation. "Thinking at its best," he went on, "goes beyond human consciousness into the strings and chords of deep space, where an eternal library of existence resides in all things. The ability to perceive is nothing more than the ability to see God's work at a single point in time. If you could imagine forever being a perfect circle, you can imagine mortality being a very rare and random crease in that perfect circle. We are a beautiful mistake in the curvature of endlessness. And, whether we believe it or not, we are all things, and all things are us. We are divine and trapped until we are released into an infinitely infinitesimal convergence of space and time and matter—a place where there's anarchy in the laws of physics, where a perceiver isn't there to regulate those laws. The universe needs an audience because we are the eyes of God and we create what we discover, and we discover what we create. And at that moment, we shed our religion and we view consciousness for what it really is—the ultimate lawmaker of biblical proportions. We can say goodbye to God as we knew Him before. 'Bye, God,' I say. 'Bye, God,' I say. 'Bye, God,' I say.

"Lawwddd, what garbage," Geneva said and turned the TV off.

"You don't like those people downstairs?" I asked.

She laughed. "Nahhh, itz jusss . . ."

"I don't like them either."

"Mr. Oscar, ya don know dem."

"They're strange."

"Dat dey are."

"Can I stay here with you?"

"Duzzz Mrs. Jeanne know ya here?"

"She knows I'm looking for you."

"We'ze be gettin' back den."

"Can we stay here? Until they leave."

"Nahh."

"I know you don't like them."

"Itzz not dat I don't like dem."

"Then what is it?"

"Itzz hard to explain, Mr. Oscar. You see, I've worked a looong way to get here, right where I am. And dose peoples—they be a-comin' ready to take. Mrs. Jeanne is fragile right now. Mrs. Jeanne ain't know whut she wants. Mrs. Jeanne feels bad 'bout herself. You see, Mr. Oscar—"

"I don't want them to be here, and I'm worried they will."

"Naaht to troubla ya. But dose two. Dose two will, surely. I can promise dat."

I began to cry.

"Ahhhh naaah, Mr. Oscar. Come on now."

"You guys up there?" I heard my grandmother call from the garage.

"We'zz be gettin' goin'."

"Yes," I answered.

"Come on down," she said.

I went down the stairs in that loud way that only kids go down the stairs.

"Geneva," I called from the bottom of the staircase.

"Be down soon and ready," she responded. "Wantz to be bringin' down da TV realz quick."

"Need help?"

"Nahhh, nawt a big TV. Mrs. Jeanne been wantin' me to trash this for a-while. Gotzz a new one been sittin' in da house I'll be bringin' over later."

"Okay. I'll leave the door open to the garage."

"Okay, thank ya."

I waited outside with my grandmother and that couple. My grandmother wanted them to say goodbye to Geneva before they left. Everyone was in good spirits and my grandmother had a look of total relief.

"Geneva," my grandmother called out again. She could see Lez was getting impatient.

"Jeanne," Lez then said. "He's in pain."

"Geneva," my grandmother called again.

"Comin'," Geneva called back.

"Okay. Lez and Rudge are leaving, and they wanted to say farewell."

Geneva made her way down the stairs, and I skipped over to grab the TV from her.

"Ahh, just putz it here," she said to me, "near tha garbage."

"Garbage?" Lez belted with fierce morality.

"Yezz?" Geneva asked back.

"You're throwing that away?"

"Yezz?"

"That's a good TV."

"Itz broke."

"Rudge fixes everything. We let nothing go to waste."

Lez picked up the TV from the garage floor and brought it over like she was holding an abandoned baby.

"You can always fix things," she went on, scolding Geneva.

"Screenz half broke. Yaaa couldn't get five dollas fer dat."

"Five dollars! That's a lot of money. That's close to a whole hour my poor Rudge works in a hot kitchen. They have no fans in that kitchen. His health benefits are horrible, and I pay out of pocket. His deductible is through the roof—might as well not have insurance at all."

"Yuuzz always sick or somthin?" Geneva punched back.

"They have him working in a hot kitchen and if something happens to me, I pay thousands. I don't have thousands. And he already pays thousands."

"Makin' five dollas an hour?"

"So," Lez ignored, "so when I see a TV like this being thrown away, I can't help but think it's being wasted. See our little yellow Beetle over there? See Torrance?"

"Torrance?" Geneva asked, laughing to herself. "Whuuuz Torrance? Yuuuz gotta dog in der name Torrance? I see a whole lotta luggage. A dog tucked in dat luggage?"

"No, I don't. We don't. Torrance is my car. We care about the things we own, and we make them last. We named our car. We love our car. That's why we called him Torrance. See, we treat our car like a person."

"Or ya'd treat a person like a car."

"Excuse me? It's not a 'car.' It's a 'him.'"

"Him?"

"Yes, since his name is Torrance, I refer to him as 'him.'"

"Datz nice."

"I'm glad you think so," she hissed between her teeth. "A whole hour of my poor Rudge in a hot kitchen with bad insurance," she then said to herself as she tried to stuff the TV into her little yellow Beetle. "You know," she added through this backbreaking work of putting the TV in the car, "I think you would appreciate this—I took one of those DNA tests. I'm part Egyptian and I'm part—"

"Datz nice," Geneva interrupted.

"You don't care?"

"Honey, yuuuz a bottle of wine?"

"Ummm. A bottle of wine?"

"Then, honey, why Ize care where you from . . . ?"

That is how Geneva and the odd couple said goodbye. My grandmother was too relieved to know what had even happened and she waved to them in her trance from the driveway. Their car sped down the road and no brake lights illuminated to show they slowed down at the intersection. Seeing brake lights was always a part of the experience of seeing someone leave the property. It always made me sad to see those red lights flicker and to turn around and reacclimate myself to the quiet of the house and the woods around it. Even if it was a bad guest, the land lost life when people exited it.

◆

The land where Lez and Rudge would live was torn apart. The process took longer than my grandmother had thought, and the beautiful lawns were uprooted to bury the pipes that would connect their house to the main water well. A new generator was put in for both houses because Lez refused to buy her own generator. She wanted to live off the main house as much as she possibly could.

Close to a year after they first visited, the odd couple moved into their new home. Lez called it the *double-wide* because it still made her a victim to the world—her, the oppressed and my grandmother, the oppressor. Lez could never admit that someone was kind enough to build her a house for free and furnish it for free—*everything* for free. There was zero cost to them. Utilities, covered. Rent, covered. All profit. No expenses. What a life. But they didn't make it seem that way. Because Lez said it was the double-wide. And she could always make my grandmother feel bad using that word. And she had a certain tone in her voice every time she wielded it. When her friends came over, she would ask my grandmother if she could use our kitchen because the "double-wide" wasn't big enough for company. My grandmother felt so embarrassed by it and would leave the house to go shopping so she didn't have to show her face to Lez's friends. She would be gone for hours and, of course, Lez and her friends would still be there when she got back. I would watch that old limping woman tiptoe over to the pool to get some sun to avoid the shame she'd experience inside her own house. I was in the kitchen once when this happened, and it was almost pathetic to witness.

"She's back," one of Lez's friends said—she was a maverick podcaster. She was one of the crew. All of them were there right now. They were such loungers. And they draped their bodies about with an indifference of their present and a genuine misunderstanding of the fact they were guests in someone else's home. There was a total lack of self-awareness. A lack of grace. A lack of dignity. It was "me in the moment" with all of them. And they could be so unbelievably rude. And so self-righteous. And vicious. So vicious when they wanted to be. Like a snake suddenly striking out of nowhere with the venom spirting from its mouth. These were dangerous, unhinged people. And they never held back when I was around. Adults never do when kids are there. Guess I was quiet and nonthreatening. Like a dog, *Oscar couldn't say anything even if he wanted to*, I assumed she thought. I bet she did. Can't prove it. But I would bet my life on it.

"At the pool again?" Lez asked, too tired to look out the window.

"What a guess," the podcaster laughed.

"*Goyishe kop*," Lez whispered to herself, smiling in an almost demonic way.

"What's that?" the podcaster asked.

"Oh, nothing. Just something about brutal old White women. They don't stand a chance."

"A chance for what?"

"People like us."

"That's right—because we don't take crap from no one."

"Exactly. Hey, you still a part of that dog-with-three-legs charity thing?"

"Yeah. Why?"

"My friend found a cutie."

"Three legs?"

"That's the thing. He has four."

"Only three legs."

"He needs a home, too."

"Three legs."

"You and your rules."

"Three legs."

"Just because you're an authority in your own world doesn't mean you have to be an authority in mine."

"Three legs."

"I hear ya. I hear ya!"

"Rules are rules. You have to be firm and belligerent to be ahead of your time."

"And you are?"

"Yes, I am. Those four-leg dogs can find a home somewhere else. They don't have it as bad as the three-legged ones."

"You're not the only one ahead of their time. I am."

"We all are. That's why we're friends."

"It's a burden," Lez sighed.

"You said it, girl."

"So much wrong around us."

"Mmmhmmm."

"We go forward and everyone else goes backward."

"That should be a quote."

"I am quotable."

"You are, Lez."

"A lot of people have said that. I should write a book."

"I would read it."

"Many others, too. One day. I have a lot to say. I need to be heard through all this wrong. It's the world that's holding me back. It's holding us all back because we're too ahead of our time."

"Speaking of too ahead of their time . . . you know Maggie?"

"Yeah," Lez answered.

"She was in the paper."

"No way," Lez suddenly shrilled. "For what?"

"She had that wildly successful coffee shop in the city. Turns out it was wildly successful because she wasn't paying her employees."

"You've gotta be kidding."

"Nope. As serious as can be. She didn't pay a lot of them. I saved the paper. I have it at home. I'll show you. Allegedly she had some working double shifts without compensation. One person claimed to have worked a full twenty-four-hour period with eight hours' worth of pay."

"I can't even . . ."

"Yeah, and it gets worse. Maggie fired that employee for complaining. The day after she worked twenty-four hours straight."

"Wait . . . they're open through the night, too?"

"Yes. That was her whole thing. A coffee shop for the people who go to school during the day and work at night. Remember—'the coffee shop for the common man'?"

"Not ringin' a bell."

"Come on, Lez. She was pretty big."

"Maybe I was in there without even realizing. I'm a busy bee, ya know. Don't know where I am half the time. Probably stumbled in and stumbled out with the phone glued to my ear."

Lez would continue to inject that self-importance into her veins as she pretended not to know this successful woman. I could tell she hated women who she felt had the upper hand. She was angered by the fact she wasn't the one who thought of the insomnia coffee shop. Her demeanor told me this.

"Maggie was also a busy bee."

Lez's face dropped, dead with jealousy. "I'm sure she was."

"Very busy. Had a few breakdowns. The work was killing her. It's hard to run a business all on your own. I feel bad for her."

"Not the employees?" Lez hissed.

"Yes, of course them, too."

"Wasn't Maggie a big union activist?"

"She still is."

"How does that make any sense?"

"Why?"

"She treated her employees like shit and she's a union activist at the same time."

"She's not a union activist for her shop."

"Do you hear yourself?" Lez cried.

"What?"

"It makes no sense what you're saying. You're contradicting yourself."

"Am I?"

"Yes."

"I don't think so."

"You are."

"Anyway. Maggie's lawyer really has her back."

"What does that mean?"

"Well, you know Maggie is bipolar, right?"

"No, I didn't know," Lez fumed, her eyes fluttering in panicked anger.

"I spoke to her the other day, and she said her lawyer may be able to build a great defense case out of that."

"Being bipolar?"

"Yes. Wait . . . I think it's that. Or maybe it was an anxiety disorder?"

"Anxiety disorder?"

"Yes. That's it, I think."

"How does she have an anxiety disorder?"

"A fear of heights, I think."

"How would you know that?"

"Maggie said. I was so curious what she was anxious about."

"Isn't everyone anxious about heights?"

"But hers is bad. Very bad."

"How bad?"

"If she's looking out from the window of a very tall building, she gets sick to her stomach."

"Vomits?"

"No. She feels scared, and her stomach turns, I think. I'm trying to remember how she said it exactly."

"That's how I feel. I think that's how everyone feels when they look out of a window from the top of a skyscraper."

"Oh my gosh. Then maybe you also have that anxiety disorder."

"Me and the rest of the world?"

"Okay, Lez. Let's not be ridiculous now. And let's not make fun of people with disabilities. You know, I can't take the risk of being seen around backward people, Lez."

"Wouldn't want that."

"No, I wouldn't."

"It would be contradictory."

"Yes, it would."

"Like Maggie."

"Don't be—"

"If it is wrong now," Lez interrupted with sudden inspiration, "was it wrong then?"

"What?"

"You heard me."

"I don't understand the question, Lez."

"Think about it."

"What does this have to do with anything?"

"Of course, it's wrong then," Lez answered her own question. "But what can you do about it now? Erase the past? Keep it living and expose it for what it is and learn from that and so on . . .? I say burn it all. Start it back up the right way with us leading it the right way. The day we were born is the day it all really starts. And it's tasked for us to build it back up from here on out. It's our universe now to take ownership of. Our life for others to follow. Time to snap and fold reality into whatever we want, girls. Let's build it up, bitches."

"It gets me thinking, actually. They want to bring *Dumbo* back."

"So what?"

"I would never watch a racist production."

"How's it racist?"

"You're kidding... watch it again. All the Disney stuff is racist. *Peter Pan*, come on, Lez. Watch it and see for yourself. It disgusts and offends me."

"You think we should ban these movies?"

"Hell yes. Each and every one of them."

"I know where you stand. And that's why I love you. Though, you have to admit *Dumbo* is beautifully done."

"I would rather have bad artistry that's politically sound than good artistry that's not."

"God, I love you. Curious... what do you think of the Grinch?"

"You mean the Dr. Seuss character?"

"Yeah."

"Don't even."

"What?"

"Don't even get me started on that. We all know he's the outcast because he's green. Different than all the other Whoville people."

Lez was shaking with pleasure. She almost stuttered.

"My sentiments exactly."

The wheels were spinning now, and Lez let this podcaster ambulance-chase her own momentum.

"It's just sooo disgusting. To poison the minds of children with this inherent racism. They condition them to hate minorities. It's a horrible, deplorable thing that's happening. Our poor children. Brainwashed. I'm going to make a viral anti-Disney campaign. You'll see, Lez, after I'm through the only Dumbo people will know will be the one in Brooklyn."

Lez moaned now. She got off on this brewing activism.

"I will stand behind you."

"I hope you will. I hope everyone will. For the sake of society and our children. I'm only thinking of the children. Only the children."

The podcaster star began to cry.

"Oh, sweetheart, what?" Lez asked.

"Nothing. Nothing. It's just . . ."

"Come on, sweetie, tell us."

"I don't want to do this to myself again."

"Do what?"

"Get my hopes up. And then nothing happens. It's hard to go viral."

"I have a firm belief in you. We all do."

"I know. I know. But I've been here before. My therapist says I need to stop being something to everyone else and be something more to myself."

This statement hit some deep untouched nerve in Lez.

"What the fuck kind of comment is that? Total bullshit. Don't listen to it. It's our *job* to be everything to everyone else. We are symbolic. That's the burden we bear. That's what the past has done to us. That's what it made us be. Don't let some 'therapist' tell you otherwise. The therapist isn't a part of what we're trying to do. You're either in or out. That therapist is out."

"I don't know, Lez."

"You don't know?"

"She told me a story once. About a young boy who turned eighteen. He got a sex change operation and killed himself three years later. She told me he did it because he wanted to be relevant. He felt he had nothing to show for his life and this was his way to be seen and appreciated. She described it as 'having all the lights on you.' That's how I always feel when I want to go viral. All the lights are on me. Like they are now. And then, after some time, it gets quiet. Those lights turn off. Everyone has walked away from you. And you have to deal with what you've done in silence and alone and in the dark. It isn't until then that you know the truth. And I think that's why the poor kid killed himself three years later. Because he realized he was never anything to himself. He was just a statement piece yearning for the immediate attention and admiration."

Lez's anger steamed up into a sudden calm. You saw the lightning and you were wondering when the thunder would come. It never did.

"Then don't."

"Then don't what?"

"Don't go viral. Don't stand for something. It's up to you."

"That's not fair, Lez."

"Oh, but it is. It's your life. Your choice. Do as you please. We live in a *free society*." Lez hooked her back into it with "a free society."

"It's very much not a free society, Lez. There's injustice everywhere—all around us, yearly, daily, hourly . . . by the minute!"

"All right then."

"And it's up to us."

"Yes, it is."

"If it's not us, it's no one."

"Truer than true."

"What am I thinking? I have a voice!"

"You do. You sure do."

"I'm not a flash in the pan."

"You're sure not. You're the forest fire."

"Yes, burning through Napa Valley so those rich people can't get their three-hundred-dollar bottle of wine."

"And what are you to the poor?"

"I'm the rain so they can have more water."

"What did Professor Nelson teach us?"

"If you aren't screaming, you're not making a sound."

"Right."

"Thank you, Lez."

"I love you, sweetheart."

"Love you, too."

"Oh, oh, oh!" Lez screamed.

"What? What? What?"

"We gotta go to the city next Thursday."

"Why?"

"You know why. That new bakery that opened on the west side. They say it has the best double chocolate chip cookie, like, ever made in the history of the world."

"What time are you going?"

"We're going. All of us. Eight a.m."

"I won't want a cookie at eight a.m."

"Not to eat it. To have it. You can eat it later. Don't you want to be able to post about it?"

The podcaster's eyes lit up. "All right, eight a.m. it is."

"Perfect."

"Oh, crap."

"What?"

"I think I was supposed to go to that super-impossible-to-get-into brewery in Charlton, Massachusetts."

"On Thursday?"

"Yes. I have to go. Eva would kill me if I didn't. She got me a ticket."

"You need a ticket to go to a brewery?"

"Yes. She got these tickets months ago. Otherwise, you wait in line for like hours. Well, you still wait with a ticket. It's a much shorter line. They make the best beers in the world, I hear."

"I think the best cookie in the world is better than the best beer in the world."

"But I already told her, Lez. How long is the wait at eight a.m.?"

"Could be hours."

"I'm sorry, Lez."

Something made a vibrating sound in Lez's pocket, and she ripped out her phone.

"It's here," Lez jumped up and down. "It's here!"

She ran out of the kitchen and through the front of the house. I heard her kick the door open and heard it smack back closed. I watched her take the package from the delivery guy. She would never say thank you. The guy shook his head after she violently grabbed the package from his high-friction gloves. She nearly took his arms with her as she ran back in like a child.

"Well . . ..?" the podcaster asked, so intrigued.

"It's here!" Lez screamed in her kiddish, selfish madness.

She pulled the item out of the box. It was a pair of socks.

"All this for socks?"

"Not just any socks. Totally recycled. These are so sought after. Totally sold out now. Next supply isn't for a few months. I think they're made out of plastic straws. Yes, see the turtle logo. Each pair saves a turtle."

"I love the logo. And I love that you saved a turtle."

"It's cute, isn't it. Oh, and look at this!"

She showed everyone in the kitchen a picture of the turtle she saved. What a marketing gimmick. But brilliant. Lez read the note from the turtle:

"'Dear Lez.'"(The "Lez" part of this note was made to look handwritten. Really a good typeface. And there was an underline under the "Lez.")"'Dear Lez. It's because of you I'm alive and well. Living my best days in Costa Rica. Love, Nesty.'"

"Oh my gosh, Lez. What a cute little name."

"I care. See, I care."

"You do, Lez. You do care."

Lez began to cry out of love for herself and that little turtle that had the ability to write notes. I was convinced she got the socks solely because she liked the logo more than anything else.

"I care so much," she sobbed from self-amazement.

"But, Lez, try not to buy so much stuff."

Lez sucked back up the tears and the anger settled in with a dry ferocity.

"This is *stuff*? Saving poor Nesty's life so he can live freely in Costa Rica?"

"It's still a production of superfluous goods."

"It's saving the environment."

"Lez, you know as well as I do services rather than goods is the economy of the future. You know this from Professor Nelson. Even though it's to save Nesty, those socks are still a production of superfluous goods, which produce more waste. Invest in the experiential, as he taught us. That produces zero waste."

"I'm buying these socks to get rid of the straws in our oceans. Can't your little mind get that?"

"Lez, I'm a messenger. Don't get angry at the messenger. You know what Professor Nelson taught us."

"Yes, yes," Lez said, "Professor Nelson. Many lifetimes ago. I'm surprised you still remember him. Gets me thinking, though... you're getting a dog, aren't you?"

"Probably. Why?"

"You should get him, her, they, them on that NutritionForLife diet."

"I've heard of that."

"I have a friend who works for the company. High up."

"That's the one hundred percent organic pet diet, right? That pet program is a fortune. All local ingredients. Fresh wild-caught fish. Free-range chicken. The food is different each time you get it. Only the most natural ingredients."

"Kobe beef only, I'm sure of it. The best of the best. From Japan's Hyogo Prefecture. Strictly following the guidelines of the Kobe Beef Marketing and Distribution Promotion Association. Even better than the old crap that oppressor out there drops off at our door. My sweet husband comes back from a hard day of work to a pound of Boar's Head deli turkey. Can you imagine? Asking for colon cancer. I don't know how she doesn't have it. She'll go out and shop for herself and bring us that stuff back thinking it's real nice. It just shows what she thinks of us. Boar's Head. How horrible. She's a Boar's Head. And I... I don't even acknowledge we got anything. I just give it to the crows. Leave it by that crumbling doghouse behind our double-wide for the crows."

"How do you even get invited?" the podcaster ignored, enamored by this super-premium and special pet food.

"You either wait forever and probably never get in. They never reject you. They just don't call you back—*ever*. Or . . . you have to know someone like me. I can get you in."

"You'd do that for me, Lez? I don't know—sometimes I feel . . . like this is all . . . well, a little vain, you know. I get a little shy with it, sometimes."

Lez rolled her eyes and put on that patronizing Dr. Seuss storytelling voice. "Oh dear. Everyone's vain. You're not above it. You're in it. Nothing is genuine. Because even being genuine is still a statement. You can't escape those statements. You can't complain about them. That's like someone complaining about the traffic when they're in the traffic. You are what you hate."

The podcaster didn't respond. She sensed a truth in what Lez said.

"Of course," Lez continued, knowing she had successfully educated her friend. "Of course, I'll get you the pet food. I'll call her up tomorrow. I'll say you'll give her a call when you decide to get the pooch."

"You're not tricking me, Lez?"

"Can you shut up about that? You act so . . . it's just so embarrassing to witness when you act like this."

"I'm—"

"You're so *cheugy*."

"Cheugy?"

"Yes, cheugy."

"What is that?"

"You don't know?"

"Never heard of it."

"Look it up. Anyway, I know who came up with that word."

"Wow. Who is it?"

She paused and you could tell she didn't know this person. "I'd Rather not," she responded.

"Bad boyfriend," the podcaster laughed.

"How do you know it's a man?"

"I don't."

"Exactly. So don't generalize. And it may be a 'they.'"

"I didn't mean to offend."

"Well, you did. To assume things like you do."

"I'm so sorry."

"Enough. Anyway, did you watch that movie?"

"Oh, yes!"

"What did you think?"

"*Jeanne Dielman*, right? You're talking about that?"

"*Jeanne Dielman, 23 Quai du Commerce, 1080 Bruxelles*," she corrected.

"Right. Honestly—"

"Yes?"

"Kinda boring. A lot of doors being opened, and lights being switched on and off. Don't you think?"

"If I thought that, why would I suggest it?"

"Well . . ."

"Wouldn't make much sense."

"I suppose not."

"So, you don't like films about the struggle of women in a male-dominated world."

"You got that from *that*?"

"I have a brain."

"It's long."

"And I have an attention span."

"It was soothing."

"Soothing?"

"Yes. Kinda like that ASMR stuff. Very sensory with all the opening doors and the lights turning on and off."

"ASMR?"

"Yes."

"That's what you got from it—a sensory experience?"

"Yes. It's the greatest film ever made. You know that?"

"Is it?"

"It is."

"Remember that line that one guy told us—remember, at the bar . . .?"

"Which bar?"

"The one. I can't remember it. He had a great line—and then I slept with him. Haha."

"There's a lot of those."

"I know. I know. But I'm talking about this one."

"Oh. 'Only a coward can write a hero. Because a hero doesn't have time to write.'"

"Oh my gosh—yes!"

"I can't believe you fell for that."

"He was so Hemingway."

"The guy was a loser. An accountant or something. Pretended to be a Navy SEAL."

"But he was hot though, SEAL or not. Come on. You can't deny that."

"They can't all be hot."

"I love all men."

"One small step in between your legs . . ."

"That's a little . . ."

"What?"

"Nothing."

"What?"

"Rude."

"I can't express myself?"

"Not by offending me."

"That's how I express myself."

"Okay. Okay."

"I just can't believe that masterpiece of a film did nothing for you—you know, being a woman. How it captured us in this world of men."

"It was kinda . . ." the podcaster attempted to explain herself. "Kinda like . . ." she tried again.

"I'm more," she went on, "more into *The Godfather.*"

"*The Godfather*?"

"Yeah."

"Men shooting men—how original."

"I mean it's more than that."

"Are you a housewife—like that old relic out there by the pool?"

"Excuse me?"

"Are you?"

"I'm not and I don't know if she is either. She's a property owner."

"Housewives don't own their property?"

"It's the way you're saying it."

"No. No. You're the one who's drawing assumptions on the way I said it. I was just asking a simple and direct question."

"It's not simple and direct with you."

"I take offense to that."

"I've taken offense to almost everything you say to me."

"Well, you deserve it. And I need to vent. My doctor tells me I do. And I'm sorry it's you. But I need to do it for my health."

"I don't give a damn."

"Clearly. About all us women, too."

"I thought you didn't identify as a woman?"

"I don't identify as a woman when people categorize me as a woman."

"What does that mean?"

"It means I don't like being called a woman, but I do see myself as one."

"How am I supposed to understand that?"

"You wouldn't. And that's why I don't expect that much out of you."

"You're a—"

"What?"

"You know."

"Say it—objectify me more."

"Such a—"

"Cunt?"

"You—I would never use that word. A disgusting word."

"You thought it."

"You can't tell me what I'm thinking. You know, you act like a little king."

"Ahhh. But not a queen. Because queens are subservient to kings. Right?"

"Go shove it. You can be such a bitch. *That* was the word. Not cunt."

"Another great word to describe women. Keep objectifying."

"Why are you so angry?"

"How am I angry?"

"Look at what you're doing."

"I need this," Lez growled.

"I'm sorry about not liking the film—or maybe just not getting it."

"I understand. It went over your head. Art can do that."

"I like *Casablanca*—love it, actually," the podcaster tried to redeem her artistic and worldly self.

"Two White people in love. Original."

"I wouldn't say it's just that."

"It's just that."

"You have World War II. That's more than just two White people."

"That was a White person's war."

"What?"

"And we don't even know if the Holocaust even happened."

"That—"

"You hear what they say about it."

"I just can't . . ."

"I'm not making this up. I suppose the next movie you'll mention is *The Searchers*. That's the most racist movie of all time."

"I think I saw that way back."

"The way they treat those poor Indians," Lez said in her patronizing baby voice.

"Indians . . . ?"

"Yes. Indians."

The podcaster had the upper hand now. The fabric of Lez's moral superiority was starting to unweave, and the podcaster would pull on that thread until the whole thing unraveled. This could be defeat.

"Lez," she announced. "They aren't called Indians. They are called Native Americans."

Lez went white. *Shit*, I imagined her thinking. She reminded me of the Grinch when he was caught by Cindy Lou Who. She had to think of something fast. But she did. Because, like the Grinch, she was way more cunning than her opponent.

"You are so *meta*," Lez struck back.

In their world, *meta* was the worst thing you could say about someone. It was a more intense way of calling someone a hypocrite.

"How on earth am I *meta*?"

Success. The podcaster could no longer smell the blood from the wound. Lez was in the clear.

"You are and you know it."

"No, Lez, I don't."

"Well, who cares really?"

"What?"

"Who cares when basically the world's ending."

"All right."

"No, seriously. You heard the news about that bomb cyclone coming?"

"I have no idea what that is."

"It's a bad storm. And these atmospheric river storms. The world's trying to get rid of us. We're like little viruses on it and it's trying to fight the infection."

"I never thought of myself as a virus. Wait a second. I remember hearing about that now. Isn't that big storm going to hit somewhere in the Midwest? I don't think it's going to be a problem here."

"Well, I'm sure we'll get part of it. And that old relic out there wants me to still *work* in the middle of the bomb cyclone. I told her about it, and she said the property has surely seen far worse weather. Told me how the family would wait at the stairs in case the house got struck by lightning. Barns would burn down or something like that. How they never had lightning rods in the old days. So, I told her that her generation had never seen weather like this. No response to that. She clearly could care less about the environment. I mean she caused all of this and now she doesn't care about it. If we can just get rid of the older generations and move on with more understanding and caring people . . . then just maybe things would be just a little better for the future."

"Everything's in a panic—can't disagree with you."

"For a good reason. We're not wanted anymore. We've done so much harm. Earth hates us. Well, not us. More of the old people like her who imprison their 'help' and make them work in bomb cyclones and atmospheric rivers."

"I do get depressed by it. Then I binge that show to take the edge off."

"Oh my gosh, which one?"

"I know. So many, right?"

"Which one?"

"*Succession*."

"Oh my God. That show is amazing. Totally amazing."

"I kinda love the misery."

"That's exactly why I watch it. Seeing rich people be miserable—it doesn't get better than that. And the way they talk. So bizarre. But so brilliant."

"I know, right?"

"Totally. It almost recharges you to see their misery."

"I feel bad about it. Because who wants to see suffering, no matter who it is."

"Oh, get over yourself."

"Get over myself . . . ?"

"Yes."

"I was—"

"Stop feeling bad for all your faults."

"What are you talking about?"

"It's always about you. It's always about the guilt you have."

"Lez, it's not funny, okay?"

"Who said it was funny?"

"You know what I mean."

"Speaking of funny. You know what my uncle said to me?"

"What did your uncle say?"

"He said our generation has no sense of humor."

"I would agree."

"You think I have no sense of humor?"

"It's not just you—it's a whole generation."

"But I'm a good representation."

"You could be funnier."

"Funnier?"

"Yes. We all could be."

"How would that work?"

"I don't know . . . maybe if we didn't feel like we're always offending someone or something like that."

"So, you want to go back to the old ways and be offensive. Listen, I would rather be boring than funny if it means I'm a better person for it."

"Guess so."

"You have a lot of learning to do. A lot of growing up. We can't all be comedians."

"Please, Lez."

"Don't 'please' me."

"I want you to stop being so mean."

"If you can't be funny you gotta be mean, right?"

"That's a terrible way of looking at it."

"I gotta use the energy somewhere. If I can't use it to be funny, I'll use it to be mean. Be vengeful of all the wrongdoing of humanity. Use it to fight the good fight of injustice. I'll be a warrior for all of us. I'll have Rudge be my wingman. My Robin. Isn't he just so cute—that Rudge . . . ? So hardworking in that hot kitchen. For those horrible people who age him each day. He looks older and older each time he comes back."

"My cousin got half his face blown off in Afghanistan. Had to get reconstructive surgery."

Lez brushed off the comment and continued. "It's that kitchen that will kill my poor man. Poor old Rudge. Working so hard. Each and every day."

"You're supposed to work each and every day, Lez."

She brushed this off too. "Poor old Rudge. Sweet man, really. In his cute little lumberjack phase. Dresses like one. He's been in a lot of different phases. But he's always still the same hardworking man. You know, we don't get any of our clothes from mainstream brands because of the child labor stuff. We get it straight from small shops that make their own apparel. Like the butcher shop up near Livingston. They sell shirts there. I like having things only the staff has. It really helps those poor children working like Rudge does in China."

"I think those shirts are still made in China."

"False."

"Turn around."

The podcaster checked the great philanthropist's shirt collar.

"Yup," the star confirmed. "Made in China."

"Whatever," Lez fought back, shrugging the hand off her shoulder. "Make your own assumptions."

"I'm not making any assumptions."

"Oh, but you are."

"No, really. I'm not. The proof is right there."

"Is it now?"

"Yes, it is."

"You know what you are?"

"What am I?"

"A jealous little girl."

"Of who—of you? Oh, please, Lez."

"You've always been. Ever since I've known you."

"You're making things up, Lez."

"A jealous little bitch."

"You're the jealous bitch—jealous of the world."

"At least I have a brain."

"You—a brain? Far from it, sistaaa."

"Fuck you."

"Who was the fourth president of the United States?"

"Who cares."

"Because you don't know. You would care if you knew."

"Aren't we all trying to forget the past? I'm sure the fourth president had a slave. And you want me to remember him?"

"Why are you assuming it's a 'him'?"

"What?" Lez squealed.

"You said 'him.'"

"I know I said that."

"Okay."

"There hasn't been a female president."

"So, now you're creating gender barriers."

"What?" Lez squealed again.

"Never mind."

I wondered if this podcaster had unexpectedly won this pointless argument.

"Listen," Lez floundered, "if you want to live in the past, live in it. I look to the future. And, you know, if anyone should look ahead, it should be you."

"Why?"
"Why do you think."
"Why?"
"What was your nickname way back . . ."
"Shut up, Lez."
"Should I tell everyone?"
"Lez."
"How about I tell everyone what you were sooo good at back in the day."
"Lez."
"Hey. Wait!"
"Yesss?"
"I totally forgot to ask."
"Ask what?"
"When you went to Copenhagen, did you go to Noma?"
"I can't believe it slipped my mind."
"Oh, you didn't go."
"No, no, no. We did. It was transformative."
"Oh my gosh!" Lez screamed and fanned herself.
"Oh my gosh!" Lez screamed again and fanned herself again.
"Oh my gosh!" Lez screamed once again and fanned herself once again.
"Absolutely delightful, Lez."
"You make me sooo jealous," Lez added. "That's an experience I always wanted. Don't you just hate when other people seem to just sap up all the experiences you just want for yourself?"
"My biggest pet peeve. My goal is to soak up as many experiences as I can. I don't care about things—objects, you know. I care about food and places—travel, you know."
"Me too. Me too. I want to suck up all the experience in this world through a straw. So, when anyone goes anywhere, I can say, 'Been there, done that.' Then when they go after me all they can think of is me enjoying what they're experiencing right then, that I was

there before them. The fact I was first means I own it. But now you own that one—you own Noma. Little bitch."

"Well, I'm not saying you shouldn't go."

"So smug."

"How am I being smug?"

"Smug little bitch."

"Go to Geranium. Fantastic restaurant in Copenhagen we didn't go to."

"Bullshit."

"It's ranked number one in the world."

"Who says?"

"It's called the *World's 50 Best Restaurants*."

"Oh, I know that. Right, right. I remember seeing that as number one on the list. Rudge and I are going to plan a trip where we go to the top ten restaurants in the world. You've been to Central in Lima?"

"No."

"Disfrutar in Barcelona?"

"No."

"Diverxo in Madrid?"

"Nope."

"Pujol or Quintonil in Mexico City?"

"Nope. Nope."

"Asador Etxebarri in Atxondo?"

"No."

"A Casa do Porco in Sao Paulo?"

"Nah."

"Lido 84 in Gardone Riviera?"

"Ummmm, nooooo."

"Le Calandre in Rubano?"

"Yes—I mean no. Nope. Nahhh."

"Thank God."

"All for you and Rudge."

"Then we'll tell you about it and give you recs."

"Sure."

"I doubt you'd know the difference, really."

"I brought you into food, Lez."

"You're kidding."

"Of course I did."

"You did not."

"Fuck you."

"No, fuck you."

"All right."

"Oh my gosh!"

"What, Lez?"

"I'm looking at my Insta and there's this *adorable* pooch."

"Oh, I know. How adorable."

"Sooo adorable."

"What's the brand?"

"It's a . . . ahhhh, Nova Scotia Duck Tolling Retriever."

"Yes!"

"Brand is from Canada."

"Made in Canada. Lez, I love those dogs. Their little noses are the same color as their fur."

"That color combination is amazing. Very rare. Sought after. I think there's always a limited run."

"The limited run gets me. It's addicting. You gotta get your hands on one when they come out."

"Didn't your friend get one?"

"Oh yeah. Of course. The dog got really fat, though. They went all the way to Canada. You don't want to get one from the USA. Like buying clothing made in China. You want it made in Canada. So, they went there. Brought it back to the city and the dog is sooo fat now. Never goes out. Just eats all day. They have busy jobs and they just really wanted to have one because they're so rare and beautiful looking. I think they're both in startups. Busy people."

"Not as busy as me," Lez hissed as she flicked her thumb across her phone screen, mindlessly scrolling. "I can't take a breath here. Slave plantation. She works me to the bone. I can barely even look at my Insta. She really has me working five jobs in one. Oh, see that?" Lez waved her phone at the podcaster.

"What?"

"If you want them . . ."

"No way!"

"Yes way."

"They're in?"

"Yup."

The podcaster flicked through her phone, her fake nails scratching and clicking against the screen.

"Oh my God!" the podcaster screamed. "They have them—in my size!"

"Hirohito Tanaka is even signing them."

"He's signing the jeans?"

"Looks like it. In the inside pocket. You finally got your first pair of bespoke raw denim jeans."

"Buy!" she screamed, vigorously clicking at her phone.

"You did?"

"Buy! Buy! Buy!" she bellowed because it wasn't working.

"It's not working?"

"Yes! Oh my God! Oh my God! It went through. Shipping to me . . . wait for it . . . in how many days . . ."

Lez started to laugh.

"Three *months*?" the podcaster cried.

"Guess you don't know Hirohito Tanaka."

"*Three months*?"

"Yup. He puts one pair up and fifty people buy it. You're one of the fifty. Now you have to wait for him to make the jeans."

"I can't wait that long."

"That's how it is with Hirohito Tanaka jeans."

"I just paid close to two grand to wait three months?"

"Yup. I did, too. For all three of my pairs. My fourth comes next week. But they're still always late."

"Late even after three months?"

"Yup. He makes them himself. He's the only one."

"I know. Makes sense."

"And for me waiting is even worse because my days are so long here. Working sunup to sundown each and every day. Slave life."

"Why don't you say something?"

"The way I see it, one day someone is going to create a series about my life on this property. Call it *Modern Slave* or something similar. Catchy, you know. The longer I wait—as I see it—the more seasons this series will have. It can only get crazier, you know... what that woman makes me do here, you know... how hard she works me. Netflix will pick this story up. I'm sure of it. This whole place is just waiting to blow up in some series finale. Popcorn out. Eyes glued to the screen. It's coming."

"I mean..." the podcaster started and stopped, almost whimpering. "I mean... Lez..."

"Out with it. What?"

"It can't be all that bad. We've been hanging out all day—aren't you supposed to work today?"

"This is my *fucking* lunch break you little cunt."

"Don't call me that. Wait... I just thought of something."

"What?"

"Don't they have that Toller dog on this property? I swear I saw it run by earlier."

"No idea."

"How do you not know? You work here."

"Fuck you."

"I'm just—"

"Shut up. I'm working too much to even notice a dog. You get me?"

"Lez—"

"You get me."

"Lez—"

"Shhhhh. You get me."

"It's so rude," another from the friend group finally chimed in, not to diffuse the situation but to satiate the boredom of listening to it.

"I'm sorry," the podcaster defended, "but our whole business model is with three legs." For some reason her mind went straight back to the three-legged dog business. After this lengthy in-between chatter, she thought about that doggy charity. These people had wandering minds to say the least. Everyone had wandering minds, really, including myself. I was to blame, too, for this lack of focus on a biblical level.

"No, not that," the other person from the friend group went on, "you notice she never comes in to say hello."

This new voice took authority in this already too-long conversation about nothing. He ponderously stalked my grandmother with his pouty face. He rested his chin on his palms, and I couldn't tell if any of the emotions he wore on his face were real. It was like some camera was on him, always. He was very flamboyant and moved about the kitchen in a light and airless way. Almost like he was doing ballet in zero gravity. He was graceful, I have to say, with those pitter-patter movements of his. "Well, no—I'm lying. She did say hi once. And you know what she said? The worst—I mean worst—way you can start off a forced conversation. She said: 'Hey, guys . . .' I can't remember the rest because I was like so, so, so disturbed by how she started it off. Like, girl. Who in these bitches are 'guys'? You know how that gets me so amped up when stupid people say that. How people generalize with that, the most backward word of all time: 'guys'? How do you know we're guys? Did we tell you? Maybe when your masculine friends invaded Normandy about a trillion years ago . . . maybe that's when they called each other "guys," but look what happened to them. Like, have you seen *Saving Private Ryan*? I don't wanna be crying to my mommy with my intestines hanging out. Not so masculine there, huh? 'Guys' is the most masculine-toxic word. It's a dominating word. You wouldn't call a group of men and women 'girls,' so why would you assume they would want to be called 'guys'? I'm sorry—but this makes my blood boil. I see red. I really see red."

"So, should we go out there and say something to the old bat?" another voice from the friend group said. It became an "I am Spartacus" moment. And this new voice belonged to a heavier-set man. He held the airless one around the hips with his arms.

"No!" Lez screamed. She enjoyed too much the place she put my grandmother in. Keeping her friends away gave her control.

"All right, Lez," the heavier-set man pulled back. "You don't have to rip my head off."

His boyfriend turned his head around and gave him a gentle kiss on the cheek. I was amazed at how far he could turn his head. Reminded me of an owl.

"Honey," this owl said, "you know how Lez can get."

"A real bitch," the heavier one laughed.

"But bitches rule the world," Lez added.

"Straight from the bitch's mouth," the owl said, slipping out of the heavier one's grip. "Oh my God. Oh! Oh! Oh! I almost forgot. Okay! Okay! Okay! I can't believe I almost forgot. Okay, so a guy I know has this company. Makes shirts, basically. I left the bag in the front. Hold on."

He ran out and the whole fragile house shook. When he ran back, it did the same.

"Okaaay," he said and dug into his bag. He pulled out a stack of folded shirts. "Look at these. Hysterical."

He unfolded one and let it hang down over his chest. Everyone laughed.

I'll get tips without no tits, it said.

He unfolded another: *ORGASM*.

Unfolded another: *Creative fucker*.

Another: *"They" isn't plural, you bigot*.

"I love that bigot one," they all said in unison with a moaning voice of praise.

The podcaster then got bored and shuffled over to a cabinet, searching for food. "You shouldn't have left the city to be in a double-wide," she said.

"I love the country," Lez defended. "I wanted to be here."

"Yeah . . . but—the conditions you live in. We can't even fit in the house that woman gave you. Doesn't it bother you she has all this land and she built you that tiny house? All this room and that's what you get out of it. And, Lez, you're taking care of this whole property. Without you . . . come on, Lez. It isn't right. You should demand more from her."

"Oh, come on. I can't. I just started."

"You can, Lez. Don't let her get away with more. If you set the precedent now, who knows how far she'll go."

The owl and the heavier one nodded their head in a very childlike way as they sucked on lollipops. I wanted one but was too embarrassed to ask. The lollipop, not them.

"What can I ask for at this point?" Lez pretended to be weak. Ears down like a dog.

"You're kidding me. Where's that bitch in there I used to know? She must've left."

"Rudge and I don't even use the dishwasher."

"Why?" they all asked in unison.

"I won't get into it."

"Come on, Lez," she begged. The other two were too proud to pry. And I don't think they cared. They just liked the heated emotion of it all. Watching was their entertainment while they sucked on those pops.

"No, I don't want to get into it."

The podcaster wouldn't woo her like she wooed her prized audiences. She would have to change the subject to avoid accepting the defeat.

"That . . . what's her name?" she asked Lez.

"Who are you talking about?"

"That woman. You know." She gestured toward Geneva's room.

"He Stopped Loving Her Today" escaped through Geneva's door. It had been on a loop for a while. They just chose to pay attention to it now. Because they felt like paying attention to it. But as they listened, I heard something else. Someone calling my name from afar. Someone crying—begging me to wake up. "Wake up! Wake up!" they begged. Then I heard another voice enter. This voice consoled the sobbing woman. I could only hear mumbling now and then, and both voices gradually disappeared. A door opened and I heard a third voice talking in a low, gargled way. I could hear him walking over to me and then suddenly a spotlight beamed right into the house through the ceiling, and no one took notice of it besides me. It moved from side to side. I had to cover my face with my hands, it was so bright. And then, like that, the spotlight went away. Now I just heard the song playing from Geneva's room. I shook my head and looked around, but the group just kept talking like nothing had happened.

"Is that a country song?" the heavier one asked.

Now they all began to whisper. It was a scandalous conversation. Loud whispering was the protocol of scandalous conversation.

"It is, you idiot," the owl said, hitting him with a lazy, playful slap.

"Stop," the heavier one moaned.

"Geneva," I finally answered for Lez.

They looked at me. And then they went back into their own spheres of gossip.

"Why would she be listening to that type of country music?" the podcaster asked. "It's sung by an old, probably racist, White male."

"White-washed," Lez answered, peeling one of my grandmother's bananas. "It's a sad reality today. Unstoppable, really."

The owl began to giggle into his palm and tried to chatter through this giggling.

"Doesn't she . . ." he tried and failed. "Doesn't she . . ." he tried and failed once again. "Oh my God," he got out. "I'm going to hell for saying this."

"What?" Lez said, angry.

"Tell us!" the podcaster added.

"She sounds off to you, doesn't she?" he asked this group of gossipers. "Like a caricature. Who the fuck sounds like that?"

They all nodded, and Lez rolled her eyes. But she was still intrigued. She just had to feel like she was above it all but would kindly give them the time of the day to hear it.

"I'm so going to hell. But—there's something kinda Roots about her."

He whisper-laughed and sucked on his pop. The heavier one snorted into his shirt to stop from laughing out loud.

"What is that?" the podcaster asked.

Lez didn't know either but wouldn't let on she didn't know. But she loved being offensive in her own fun and controlled way. And this was exactly that. Everything was a game to them, and each day was a different mode of thought with its own rules and regulations governed by them. They got a kick out of Geneva in a mean way because she sounded prototypical of another era. It was like Geneva was in some play and they hated her character. But it made for great gossip. And Lez would remain quiet until the owl answered the question.

"You've never seen Roots?" he asked, taken aback.

"Would I ask?" the podcaster snarled back.

"I guess the joke is lost on you then."

"Not on me," the heavier one said through his shirt.

"Anyway," the owl pivoted. "I'm Black so I can make a Black joke."

"And I'm Black so I can laugh at your Black joke," the heavier one said.

"Man," the owl shook its head, "it's that 'Ize be doin' dat' crap. Mastah! Mastah! Mastah! Am I right? Or am I right? I swear this place may as well be a plantation. Sooo in the past. Listen, I've always thought the rest of the world was bad, but this . . . this is fucking—the worst. Fucking Roots bad. Down to the root bad. There's racist shit written all over these old White crusty walls. I can feel it."

The owl and the heavier one laughed together in their shirts, and I watched, smiling. Society was one big cute laughable mess to them, and they were so ahead of their time that there was no one left to live in their time. The present was some sad and abandoned town in the Midwest left there just to make fun of. It was preserved to symbolize a time in history that would never die. And the owl and the heavier one spent their days walking through these types of towns, vandalizing the time-capsule memorabilia, which, in this case, was Geneva. It was easier to beat the dead horse of their chosen sundown town than it was to hop on a live one to get out. Easier to complain in a bad world than it was to achieve in a good one. That's why Lez would do everything in her power to make this good property a bad property. Because you didn't have to work hard in a bad property. If you harnessed the sympathy of those who had the aptitude to feel guilty, then you could get away with just about anything.

"Mastah! Mastah! Mastah!" the heavier one whisper-laughed through his shirt.

Lez and the podcaster looked annoyed because they weren't in the know, Lez being a lot less obvious about it than the podcaster. The podcaster wore her emotions because she was always on stage. Lez was the schemer in the shadows offstage. Lots of different personality types in this room.

"Come on, Lez," the podcaster asked for the last time. "Why won't you use the dishwasher?"

Despite the lapse of time, Lez still wouldn't budge on this. The podcaster would have to accept her defeat. But I knew why Lez wouldn't tell her. She never used any appliances in the house because she would refuse to pay for repairs. Not even someone like Lez could be ballsy enough to ask my grandmother to pay for that, too. She was smart enough to know her own limits and never took things to the point of backfiring. It was a real craft. Professional freeloading at its highest level. But she could push the envelope with her friends. By keeping them guessing, she would build her smug ego, which was only built from the sympathy of others. No one else could have it tougher than she had. If they claimed they did, they were lying and shouldn't be trusted. That's what she did with Geneva, and she managed to ruin my grandmother's relationship with her. Because Geneva was competition to Lez. How could someone like Lez be more oppressed than a Black woman? She couldn't. It was impossible and Lez knew it. The only way to succeed was to create separation between my grandmother and Geneva. And how could she do that? She could by making it very clear just how oppressed Geneva really was. And being an oppressed woman herself, Lez would know—and would sympathize and uproot all the hatred Geneva had run from down in the South. Her lack of education. The way she sounded. Why hadn't my grandmother schooled her? Why hadn't she allowed Geneva's family to live on the property? There was room, right? Tons of room. My grandmother could've built twenty double-wide homes. But why didn't she? Those ideas wormed their way into Geneva's kind mind, and it separated her from my grandmother via the reopening of old wounds formed from systemic racism. She knew what Lez was doing to her mind but the issues she was raising weren't things she could ignore.

My grandmother never offered Geneva the ability to see her family more. She knew it would distract her and it was openly said. There was no hiding behind anything between my grandmother and Geneva until Lez came to the property. Lez brought the undertones and the metaphorical hatred. That educated mind of hers. You wore this emotional armor when you were around her to thwart her education. No one was themselves when Lez was there. The real you disappeared within the layers of tropes—the tropes of Lez. In her microcosmic world, my grandmother was the typical oppressive property owner. Lez was the typical oppressed and disgruntled employee. Geneva was the typical undereducated Black cook. And I was the typical pampered and ignorant grandson. That's how it was.

To see yourself playing out some cartoonish role of someone else's script. You lived your life in Lez's mind. You were that person who fit her narrative. But we weren't as simple as that. And Lez wasn't that simple either. Not at all. She went to Columbia, I think. Majored in dinosaur studies. I thought that was cool, I admit. But what was the point? What did that have to do with caretaking? Unless she thought there were dinosaur bones buried in the ground up here and she wanted to take them for herself to sell for millions. That wouldn't surprise me. Nothing with Lez could be too farfetched. And that's what made it so unnerving to be around her. You never knew what she really thought and what she could be capable of.

My grandmother feared that. Especially since she let her into the most important place on Earth—her property. It was decaying from within. And my grandmother let the virus walk right in. It was like some bug living inside of you, day in and day out, eating off your happiness until you had no other choice but to ignore the situation by realizing the situation. There was nothing that could be done now. Lez and Rudge were here, and Geneva was on her way out. They achieved the most modern thing you could achieve; they used the failings of the past to create the failings of the future. Geneva, she was Black. My grandmother, she was White. That's all they needed to know about each other. And that's all it would become. And Geneva was a mother who needed to get back to her family in Charlotte. It wasn't her job to cook and clean for my grandmother. She was more than that. And what she did here was demeaning and inherently racist. A waste of her time. The facts were the facts. She cooked and cleaned here. And my grandmother kept her away from the ones she loved. Maybe Lez was right. Maybe she did deserve more.

◆

My memories after Lez and Rudge started working for my grandmother became a corrupt amalgamation of absurd moments. I lost the chronology of my life on that property, and that time Lez did this and that time Lez did that pinpointed time. It's sad that it happened that way. I had such beautiful memories of Mr. Wood and Geneva eclipsed by the treachery of Lez. Through her way of life, I would find myself thinking in ways I never would've thought I would. Bad thoughts. Ways of making her go away. Creative ways. This land had a darkness about it. Taken from the Native Americans, as she said. It was always the Frasers' land to me. But she made it very clear there's always a past before the past. That's hard for a kid to understand. It's hard for adults to understand. And maybe Lez was right about it. Maybe I was the problem. Maybe my grandmother was, too. I started to loathe myself, ready at moments to end my own life. I was too young to think that way. But I felt that each time I took a breath, it was taking the oxygen away from people like Lez. I was stealing from them even though she was living on our property. But that didn't matter. Because it wasn't about the facts. It was about the theory of it all. So, my emotions would sway like a tree in a storm, and I regressed into a state of nervousness propelled by my privilege. And no other day propelled my privilege more than a random Tuesday at the Grutt-Kutt gas station.

The Grutt-Kutt was about five miles away from the house, right off Gale Road. The man who owned it was Max Grutt. His wife was Alice Kutt. At least this is what I was told. There were a lot of stories up here and my grandmother loved to perpetuate them. But Mr. Grutt had the best Hostess snack selection in the country, I was convinced. My grandmother would let me roam around the store when she went, and I would pick three of the ten options Mr. Grutt usually had that day. It would start with blueberry minimuffins. My fingers would stick to the glaze on the outside and I'd dig my teeth in to penetrate the softness and the cinnamon flavors, which revealed themselves as the blueberry punched my tastebuds in the most pleasureful of ways. Five per packet. And four packets per box. From there, I ran my hands along the egg-yolk–colored metal shelves with the paint chipped in spots and the rust on the metal showing through. Much of the time my fingers would catch on these chips and blood would be drawn, and I would ask my grandmother if I had gotten the shot from the doctor. The worry of dying didn't stop me from doing this each time, in complete awe of this Hostess collection. That collection. My hands continued to run along the jagged shelves. The Donettes. A crumb-cake exterior. A spice-cake interior. Too good to be true. A union like none other. The orange-flavored cupcake. "Crème" filling cradled by a citrus cake and that squiggle-shaped tangerine icing. Orange and cream. The two would dance with each other every time I chewed on them. My hands continued to run along. Stop! The Zingers. A Twinkie with frosting. Or so you may think. It's more than that, though. You would have to try it to know what I mean. In a way, this was my favorite because its true genius was in its subtle distinction. For real pros, I mean. My hands continued to run along. Stop! The Fruit Pie. Don't worry about the apple and the lemon. Just go for the cherry. Better than any cherry pie you'd had. A cherry pie you could put in your pocket. My hands continued to run along. Stop! Suzy Q's. The oblong Hostess whoopie pie. A devil's-food cake sandwich with a fluffy and creamy inside. My hands continued to run along. Stop! Ding Dongs. First, enjoy the icing. Second, enjoy the cake. Third, enjoy the creamy heaven-filled center. This is what happened in every bite. I just broke down the experience for you. My hands continued to run along. Stop! Snoballs. Wrapped in a skin of marshmallow rolled in coconut. Below this skin, chocolate cake filled with cream. My hands continued to run along. Stop! Twinkies. We all know those. I wouldn't get those that day since Mr. Grutt always had them. Supply and demand. My hands continued to run along. Stop! This is when I really stopped. The HoHos. Chocolate cake. Vanilla cream. And chocolate icing. Swirled together like the notes of a Mozart symphony. The peak of pastry. The Grutt-Kutt gas station masterpiece and Mr. Grutt knew it and would wink at me when he had them in that day.

"You see that thing out there?" Mr. Grutt asked my grandmother.

"See what?" my grandmother replied, browsing through the aisles with her thick-knuckled hand running softly along the merchandise, her blue veins and liver spots prominent against her crepey skin. Her rings clanked against the glass Kosher Dill Claussen Spears pickle jars and scratched against the paper four-pound Domino sugar bags.

"How can you not see such a thing?" he asked and pointed out the window toward the billboard on the side of the road. "It's a hell of a thing to look at. It's the talk of the town."

"Yeah, it's a movie poster."

"Not just any movie poster."

"It says *Washington*—"

"Do you know which Washington?"

"Hadn't thought about it really. But now that you bring it up . . . I'll take a guess on George Washington."

"Exactly my point. Now, does that look like George Washington to you?"

"No, that's an African American man."

"Exactly my point. They're having a Black man play George Washington in that movie."

"I think you need to worry about other things."

"I'm worried for this country—that's what I'm worried for. When you find yourself living in a reality more fictional than fiction, you find yourself willing to bend your own perceptions because everything else is bending around you. You become the architect of your own nightmare. And that, Jeanne, gives you the ability to take the whole world down with you. We're at the end, you see—the darn forsaken end. And when I see you change the way you've changed, I know to God we're at the end."

"Poetic."

"The God's truth, Jeanne."

"What does it matter?"

"It matters a whole deal. For one, it's inaccurate."

"Maybe the story is accurate—"

"How can the story be accurate if the man himself isn't accurate?"

"Oh, please."

"It just ain't right. Misleading people like that."

"Who's being misled?"

"The children. Now they're goin' around thinkin' George Washington was Black."

"I doubt that."

"I tell you."

"I swear, you men have too much time on your hands. Such idle talk, always."

"Seems you can't even laugh about it. Larry laughed about it the other day."

"What's there to laugh about? And I never liked Larry."

"He's a bit old school, I must admit. But he's gotta good heart. You find it when you get to know him."

"It's never good when you have to find the heart."

"I say some people are a little deeper than others."

"Discovering someone is a good person only by getting to know them doesn't mean they're a deep person. It means they better work better on how they're initially perceived."

"I see," he said.

He didn't see.

"I see," he repeated. "I'm just in the mindset of having a little humor. That's all. To break up the boredom, you know? If you can't laugh, what's the point? It's just funny is all. A Black George Washington. It's just funny is all. I didn't ask for it to go up there, so I can laugh at it. It was put there, and I reacted to it. I see what I see. And when the sight is ridiculous, I have a right to laugh at it. This is my world, too. And for another thing—if we can't see things as we see them, then we're losing our senses. You understand? We lose our reasoning."

"You're saying we lose the ability to generalize."

"Well, when you say it like that . . ."

"And you want to laugh about it. I'm not sure what's funny—what warrants laughter."

"Ahh, come on now. It's funny in that it's absurd. A Black Washington. Come on now. Now, see. I got something. Gets me thinkin'. It makes me think, you know. Nothin' ain't really funny anymore. Means to say you can't really laugh no more about anything. Like I was sayin' about the senses. You can't joke. You're too worried about being a bad person for it. You're holding yourself back. That red tape. A lot of bad things are funny because they're true, you know."

"I thought they were just bad because they are bad."

"See, that ain't right. Come on now. You're talking to me. You don't have to hide behind . . . you know . . . I don't know—maybe the world just ain't a funny place no more. Oh, brother, Jeanne. You make me feel so old and so gone, you know that. Like it's all a dream or something. This town becoming a dream or me becoming some dream. Don't know which one is real. I'm guessing it's real because Kerrey is always there by my side whenever I'm home. A loyal dog. The most loyal I've ever had. Won't leave my side. I piss with her next to me. That type of loyal. And seeing that's the case, when I dream, and the dream feels like reality, I always know it's fake when my Kerrey ain't with me by my side in it. When I'm dreamin', she's never around . . . or around for very little at least . . . and nothing really adds up—inconsistency, you know . . . like time jumps—day becomes night and night becomes day . . . the narrative ain't right, even the people kinda jump around and take each other's place. Funny how that works. The little things that ground you. A dog ain't like a cat, you know. It don't just disappear like that."

He continues, following my grandmother around the store. "Anyway, I sometimes hope I'm hallucinating in a world like this. Sorry, my thoughts are all over. You'd be surprised all the craziness I see comin' in n' out of here. Gets me wild and I do wonder if I'm dreamin' up stuff—for real. I do. I do. Because we ain't livin' in any time right now. I remember the sixties and the seventies and the eighties and the nineties. They were so their own thing—so distinct. I wasn't much of anything in the fifties, so I can't say much about that.

But I do know I was distinct from my father and my mother. But what are we now? Without a definition. A big nothin'. I see people comin' in this store here lookin' like they from the eighties. Got the whole outfit. A blonde girl walked in with a Black fella. He looked like he was from the seventies. She looked like she was from the eighties. Livin' in different decades. Craziest thing I ever saw. So, the blonde took note I was staring at them both. She came off a little offended and asked if I had a problem. I'm sure it's because she assumed I didn't like her 'man.' That ain't it. Lots of Blacks come in n' out of here. I ain't care one bit. Business is business, you know. That's all it means to me. Judgment stays at home. Anyway, so she asked if I had a problem and I asked where she was from. This seemed to tick her off more, you see. She asked me why it mattered where she was from. I pulled back for sure then. Her 'man' seemed angry, crushing one of them Uncle Ben's Natural Whole Grain Instant Brown Rice boxes with his big grip. Not gonna be messin' with a six-foot-five Black fella crushin' an Uncle Ben's box. Anyways, I did notice the shoes she was wearing. Had a little star on them or something like that. A lot of women her age were wearing them comin' into this store. A lot. So, I had to ask. When I asked, she laughed at me and so did her Black fella. She told me it was better I didn't know. I asked why. She answered that I'm better off not knowing because I wouldn't be able to afford them. The Black fella laughed again with her and put the box—in a strange delicate way—back on the shelf. Now, I can't resell that box the way it was. That's a loss for me. And vandalism of property. But I didn't say a thing, being the peacemaker I am. And the Blacks know how to fight. So, I ain't gettin' into that over a box of rice. But I did ask one last time about the shoes. I really wanted to know, you know. They looked like something from the eighties. So, she did finally answer me as her man kicked the door open, cracking the glass a little. 'You'd have to lay a golden egg to get these Golden Gooses,' she says. What in the name, right? So, I looked up goose shoes and 'Golden Goose' came up. And I just couldn't believe it. Six hundred dollars for a pair of shoes. Six hundred. For sneakers. This world is crazy. People dressin' the decades like it's Halloween. Every day, Halloween. No talent anymore, simply identity exploration with little to show for. And, Jeanne, I tell you this. About the vandalism. And how I've been treated by these people. A victim. And you still look at me in that way. Like I'm somethin' I'm not. But I ain't. I just feel like crud. Alls I know . . . alls I know is I feel old and irreverent . . . what's the word? Not irreverent. I feel irrelevant. That's what I meant to say. Some old man stuck in old ways. Jeanne, you're making me feel that more than ever now. The youth do it to me, too, but you're kicking me while I'm down in this one here. I don't know—maybe the world just ain't a funny place no more. Maybe it ain't."

"Maybe it isn't."

"What I'm getting at . . . what I'm tryin' . . . well, I'm sayin'—listen, if I see a Jew saving money, over and over again, and a Black being lazy, over and over again . . . it ain't fictitious. It's there in front of me. And I draw my opinions out of what I see. And I can also laugh about it and joke about it, if I choose to do so. I didn't ask to see it. I didn't ask to see it so I could tell a joke about it."

"When have you seen this? I'm curious."

"The other day, in fact. A Hasid walked in—a lot of Hasids come in—and he filled his basket up. And he come over and he looked over the receipt for a good minute. Then he tried to correct me, saying I added something to the charge. I've been doing this for a while—I don't add things on accidentally or deliberately. I'm a moral man. And this is my town. I would never spread immorality. This is a small business. I was offended. But this didn't just happen once with the Hasids. It's happened many times. Checking the receipt. Them thinking I'm trying to take advantage of them and steal their money. Then, actually today, a Black rolls in. She's in one of them electric wheelchair things. She rolls in and I see her stand up better than ever to grab some bread on the top of the shelf. I couldn't believe it. I thought her legs didn't work. But she just didn't want to walk. A

Black man did the same thing the other week. But they never check the receipt. That's for sure. Only the Hasids."

◆

I could hear a steady beeping, setting the pace of "He Stopped Loving Her Today" by George Jones.

◆

"So, a lot of Hasids and Blacks come into your store?"

"Absolutely. The good ole White folk, less and less. I miss the days when I would have tabs here. Jimmy still has a tab. Even pays the interest if he misses comin' in on Friday to pay for the week. And he set up that interest. I didn't. You think the Hasid would volunteer to set up his own interest? The hardworking, honest people of this town are leaving. They're leaving for Montana and Wyoming. Most of my friends are going there. It hasn't been corrupted there like it has been here."

"I don't think they're going to Montana and Wyoming."

"What do you mean?"

"I think they're going to Walmart."

"That's ridiculous."

"You know who I see mostly at Walmart?"

"Who?"

"White locals. And you know what?"

"What?"

"All those lazy and cheap Whites you haven't seen at your store. Well, I've seen them at Walmart. Big fat White men and women in those electric wheelchairs. Big fat White men and women triple-checking their receipts, holding up the line, not giving a damn. Your beloved locals are at Walmart. Max, how much more, on average, do you think you charge here than Walmart?"

"Well, I don't know. That's hard to say."

"How much you think?"

"As I say, I'm not exactly sure."

"I would be very thankful you have people coming here when you charge forty percent more, on average."

"That can't be right."

"Max, I've gotten peanut butter from here and Walmart. Same brand of peanut butter. I could drive three minutes that way and pay forty percent less. But I choose not to. Just like that cheap Hasid and that lazy Black. It seems like your loyalty isn't local. Not as long as Walmart is around."

"I see what I see. And you see what you see. That's democracy."

"Right, Max."

"It is."

"You're seeing what you want to see."

"I can't control what walks or rolls through that door."

"So, you have no bias?"

"Bias?"

"You men."

"Us men?"

"This idle talk."

"Alls I'm sayin' is if we ain't allowed to see what we see, then we ain't allowed to think. And if we ain't allowed to think, we lose our ability to truly be present. That's all."

"I think you're a little too present. Less thinking may do you good."

"I can't think less with this brain," he said, knocking at his skull. "I'm stuck in this brain of mine. Always workin'. Always thinkin'. Always noticin.'"

"If you can't think beyond yourself," my grandmother sermonized in her country way, "you're only yourself. And when you're only yourself, you find out how boring it is to be yourself. And when you find out how boring it is to be yourself, you pick up a cause. And when you pick up a cause, you become a hypocrite because you can't think beyond yourself since you're only yourself. Then you hate yourself—you self-loathe. But you don't just self-loathe because you hate yourself... you self-loathe because you hate yourself for hating yourself. This is the essence of vanity. This is, in its most collective form, the end of a society."

"He Stopped Loving Her Today" began playing on the radio as Mr. Grutt's rarely seen Siamese cat ran across the counter and hid in the shelves beneath a strange painting of Napoleon dressed in rags and sitting on a chrome horse, surrounded by jugglers and clowns. Above Napoleon sits a princess in a steeple looking down at some mystery tramp who's looking back up at her with feral eyes. Carved into the princess' steeple are the words *Miss Lonely*.

"Geneva's song is playing," he said, forgetting about my grandmother's combative, sermonized insult. "How is Geneva?" he went on. "I haven't seen her."

My grandmother would have to go through situations like this throughout the town and beyond. Everyone knew Geneva and everyone knew my grandmother. It was like a king losing his queen or the other way around.

"She went back home—to Charlotte," she answered, still browsing through the aisles.

"When's she back?"

"I doubt she will be coming back."

"Well, come on now."

"Max, I think she's staying for good this time. Her family needs her."

"Who's working the farm?"

"We have a wonderful couple from the city."

"The city?"

"Yes. They're very professional."

"When I hear 'professional,' I hear 'asshole.'"

Mr. Grutt always cursed in front of me, and my grandmother didn't care.

"They're very nice, Max. And very good at their jobs. They're keeping the place running."

"Well, that's all that matters. You got a whole town that would be willing to work for you, Jeanne. You know that."

"That's very kind, Max."

"We're all here for you. Right, Osk?"

I had the three items I wanted in my arms.

"Looks like you didn't surprise me today, yet again, Osk," Mr. Grutt laughed.

I put my Hostess haul on the counter and waited for my grandmother to finish her more practical and boring grocery list. Milk, eggs, bread, cereal, lettuce, tomatoes, etc. I was glad she did it because I would never want to. Who cared about 2 percent milk versus 1 percent milk? Or whole milk? Or half and half?

"Think that just about does it," my grandmother said and put her groceries on the counter. I moved mine away so her practical junk didn't crush my HoHos.

"You seen that Lambo parked out there?" he asked. "Woman with all the kids. Six of them, I think. Bratty kids. 'Momma I want this. Momma I want that.' That sort of thing."

"Lambo?"

"A Lamborghini."

"A Lamborghini—like the car?"

"That's right."

"Six kids?"

"Right."

"That doesn't add up, Max. Aren't those cars small cars, Max?"

"I thought so too. Never saw something like that. Crazy-looking thing. So, out of curiosity, I asked the woman and she says it's a Lamborghini. They make SUVs. How about that."

"Huh. I've never seen one of those around here."

"I asked Earl about that car. He says they're all over the place now. You know Earl, don't you?"

"I do. I know Earl. For years. I had a friend that went to him a few times for repairs. Said he was good. But I know him from a few community events we overlapped on."

"He's been acting kinda strange."

"I haven't noticed."

"Opening the shop up late and closing early. He's been so negative—awfully negative. Saying these automobiles are making people sell their souls. He doesn't want to work on them no more. That's at least what he says when we grab a beer or two."

"Maybe it's the beer doing it?"

"Could be."

"But—selling their souls?" my grandmother asked. "What's that talk about? You men need a war, you know. It takes the talking outta ya."

"He goes on and on. Hunched over on the bar. Acting all crazy. Talk about how we're all losing where we came from. Directionless in this 'Lamborghini SUV world,' as he puts it. Saying kids nowadays don't know what's up from down because they don't know where anything came from anymore. That sort of type of talk. Sad talk, you know. Philosophy talk."

"Stuck between kids who don't know and old-timers who know too much. It can wear you out if you pay too much attention to either of them. There's a poison up here and it's making you men talk a lot. You're a doer, Max. You are. You built this place up and made it the market of the town. You don't need to talk like this. 'Cause that talk is for people who haven't done a thing. You understand me? You've done things. Lots of things. Don't be a talker. Between you and Marshall Matches up at that hunt club of his. The old man, Marshall—chatter, chatter, chatter. Immobile talk. Worst type of talk. Talk to pass the time. I swear, all the men . . . what's happening to you? You're all talking more than the bridge-playing women do. What in the name is going on with all y'all with that immobile talk of yours?"

The bell jingled and the door opened.

"Hey-yo, Max," a heavyset man called out. He walked with a cane and his left leg bent in.

"Billy," Max said, opening his arms. "How's it?"

"Can't complain. Can't complain. Got my Newports?"

"Yeah. One pack?"

"The wife, she'll kill me if I get two. Supposed to quit."

"I'm sure she'll kill you before the cigarettes do."

The heavyset man had a whistling raspy laugh. "That's what I tell her. I say, 'Woman, you're gonna kill me anyway.'"

"You say it as it is, Billy. Always have."

"Hey, you gotta check out this burger joint. I had a job in Midtown and a few of my guys took me to a food truck on 62nd and Madison. The most incredible burger I've ever had. Kinda like the Big Mac—but real. I wouldn't think any less of you if you just drove down there to have one. It's that good. Gotta get a classic Coca-Cola with it. Wash that juicy meat down with some good old sugar bubbles."

"I haven't been to the city in ages. Better than Friends or Blanch's?"

"Much. Ten times. Blanch's had the diner burger. It's different. Dryer by nature. Friends is good. A little more gourmet. But nothing like this. It's worth the drive. Whenever I go into the city now, I'm making all my guys take a good break to go there."

Billy threw the cash on the counter and said hello to my grandmother and ruffled my hair with his grease-stained hands. The edges of his nails were permanently discolored, and his fingers were riddled with broken blood vessels underneath those nails. The door shut.

"Billy's a good boy," my grandmother said.

"The best they come. But—Jeanne . . . Earl, he keeps saying Ferrari's even gonna make an SUV soon enough. And it's gonna—"

"Max, please. I'm trying here. Why are we still on this? Who cares about Ferrari? Who cares about any of that? You're not gonna see one darn Ferrari pull up through here—not in a million years."

"That SUV did."

"And you'll never see it again. I'm sure they were passing through. No one around here has that. And why would you care even if they did? Who cares? Really, Max. And why should Earl care? He hasn't seen one of those either. No one is bringing that type of car in to his shop."

My grandmother would focus men when they went off into the nonsensical. She was known for that in the town and the men respected her for it. In their eyes, nothing could break Jeanne. And they took her tough love because it worked. But as quiet as I was, I was perplexed in the same way my grandmother was. Max seemed to be in some type of psychosis. I think it's called psychosis. Anyway, whether I'm using the term right or not, he was under some spell and there was a deep paranoia in his tone. Like this was a murder he was telling us about. But it wasn't. This was about a random woman driving up to his store in an SUV with six kids. *The Invasion of the Lamborghini SUVs*—what a blockbuster horror.

"Yeah, you're right, Jeanne," he said with his head hanging from his shoulders. "You're right. I'm sorry. All the worrying is left on us, you know. It's been like this for a while. And as my father said, and his granddaddy said too, in a capitalistic society the burden is put on the private citizen. It's a beautiful responsibility, that burden. It's our responsibility—and only our responsibility."

"It is," my grandmother answered and took this esoteric bait. "That's small government for you."

"Sure is," Max added proudly.

"Now, Max," she went on, digging herself further into this talk she hated. "What if the government got big and still put the burden on the private citizen? What would happen then?"

"Well—darn, I don't know. Beats me, Jeanne."

Something snapped in my grandmother's resolve, and she wanted to make a point. There was so much pulling her back from doing so but I doubted she'd regain control of herself.

"What would happen if the government went, let's say,

socialist . . . and the private citizen stayed the capitalist? Would those two ever work together?"

Max scratched his head and then dug around in his ear. "Jeanne, I hadn't thought—"

"What a miserable thing that would be."

"What a miserable thing."

"To make us the enemy. That's all it could achieve."

"Right. I see."

"To make us helpless. Forever leaned on and responsible. Always responsible."

"Jeanne, you all right? You Okay?"

"Yeah . . . yes. Yes, I am."

"You sure?"

"Yes, sorry."

"No need to be sorry. Just asking if you're all right."

"Appreciate it, Max. Looking out for this old woman."

"We're old here."

"And that we are."

"I pity Oscar," Max said in throaty way. "Gotta tell ya."

They both looked at me and my eyes took on a shifty look, like a dog in trouble.

"It's his world we're living in," my grandmother commented, peering at me and shaking her head. "Ain't ours. Sure as hell ain't ours."

"The way you sound, Jeanne . . . that's the way Earl—"

"He's obviously having a breakdown," she interrupted, offended by the comparison. "There's nothing supernatural in this town, Max. It's just a classic breakdown and you're worried about him and you're trying to make meaning out of something that has no meaning. It's drunk talk. That's all. Talk you two have at bars after too many beers."

"Well . . . I don't know."

"You don't know what?"

Max looked down at a notepad he pulled out. It was full of ink. "I wrote it all down—what he said. Keeps saying things . . . things like . . . well, keeps saying he thinks about the day when a kid gets picked up from baseball practice with a Ferrari SUV. Keeps saying the kid'll only know Ferrari as the SUV and not what it was. Won't even know who Enzo Ferrari was."

"Who's Enzo Ferrari?"

"That Ferrari guy. Founder of the car company, I think."

"Max, I'm trying," my grandmother said through her teeth. She dragged her hands across her face out of frustration and her lips made a popping sound when she did that. "You gotta stop talking cars. You just need to stop, Max. For your own good. And mine."

"I'm sorry. My mind wanders. A bit scattered."

"It's all right. It's all right, Max. I want to make sure you're all right. I always do. Because I don't know what to make of all of this. We're talking about the most random stuff . . . for . . . for way too long now. You gotta get it together. Stop overthinking things."

"Yes. Yes. One last thing to say. I promise. It's just really on my mind."

"Only if it's the last of it. Please."

"He saw I was writing down his ramblings," he said, tapping the pad neurotically. "And he didn't mind me writing his words, word-for-word. And he kept going on about how these kids wouldn't know the history behind what they drive in every day. That they wouldn't care about it enough to know it. Because it's a piece of metal to them. Something that drives them to school . . . and to home . . . and to baseball practice . . . and everywhere else. He says, and I quote . . ."

He scratched his head and examined the notepad. "'We're all lost,' he said, looking even closer now. He cleared his throat and tried again. "'We're all lost in the lack of our own originality.' And then he went on to say something like amateurs see emotion as performance and professionals see performance as emotion. He cried when he said that to me. I've never seen him cry before. It was awful to see him cry. Awful. He just doesn't talk like that. Never talks like that. Never, Jeanne. I'm very worried. Very, very worried."

"Wait," my grandmother said, brushing off this heavy-handed talk. "You mean Earl senior?"

"Yeah."

"No, I know his son. He wasn't much of a talker, Earl senior. How old is he now?"

"Too old."

"Because his son must be in his mid-sixties by now. Yeah, Earl Senior was a quiet one. A bizarre one. Totally different from his son. They look different, too. Almost hard to believe they're father and son."

"Yeah, that's why I asked. I don't know if it's the old age. But the things he says now."

"It's the age. A lot of that type of talk around here nowadays."

"Never heard such talk before."

"Let it roll off," my grandmother said in her firm voice. "Let it roll off and move on."

"Holy mackerel," Max belted, pointing out the window. "See it out there?"

We followed him out the door to a red horizon. The clouds looked like blood sausages as a beet-colored glare refracted from within the enveloping fog resembling an apocalyptic hell.

"How strange," my grandmother said. "Never seen anything like this."

"Year hear that?" Max asked. "Where in the name is that coming from? You hear that?"

The red dissipated around me, and a marble staircase appeared. I found myself walking down it. The walls were a silvery blue and the lamps on these walls were bright and the fixtures were art deco in style. The pictures descended with the walls and the stairs had a simple thick black frame. I was heading down this marble staircase to go to the bathroom and I stopped at one of the urinals. The tiles on the walls depicted ancient Asian people doing various activities. One had a woman playing the flute while birds flew above her and dogs played below her. My eyes then followed the brass pipes connecting the urinals. I followed one pipe to my urinal, and it ended at a circular gold bulb with an engraved white cap on its front. The black letters arced over *LONDON W.C.* These arced letters read *DENT & HELLYER*. The urinal water came out of the bulb and the crystalline water absorbed the clean art deco light of the bathroom. I then walked over from the urinal to the sink and turned the silver four-pronged knob with a white cap in the middle of the four prongs. In the center the black letters read *COLD*. Arced around that was *BARBER WILSONS* above and *LONDON–1905* below. I washed my hands and turned the sink off and I didn't want to go back upstairs for some reason. I could see the flickering camera lights sneaking down the stairs and I could hear people screaming my first name in admiration.

Grabbing a towel, I covered my face and leaned my palms against the sink. I threw the towel in the hamper and made my way back to the marble staircase. From the bottom of the staircase, I looked up and I could see at the top a framed picture of Audrey Hepburn in a lipstick-red dress. Her hands were in the air as if she was welcoming me. But I wouldn't go up. I waited to hear my name being called from above. I saw those camera lights flickering as anticipation-driven misfire shots. Just so they could get that first unexpected picture of me returning to that hotel lobby. So I could permanently be up on that silvery blue wall next to Audrey Hepburn.

The bell jingled again, and the stiff metal door rubbed against the ribbed concrete floor. It made the most awful sound. Like rough sandpaper against even rougher sandpaper. I found myself back in the Grutt-Kutt gas station and the sky wasn't red, and we hadn't left the counter to marvel at it. I was quite in awe of myself and what had just happened.

"Piece of shit door," the woman complained, entering. Her voice sounded familiar.

"Howdie," Mr. Grutt said. You could tell he thought she was pretty.

"Right," the woman answered. She appeared from behind the first aisle and to my total distaste it was Lez. I could not imagine Lez being in a place like this. My grandmother looked more embarrassed than surprised, but she would surely find a way to trick herself into being happy she ran into Lez.

"Look who it is," my grandmother said and made her way over to give Lez a hug.

"Jeanne," Lez said in her tone that mixed rudeness and confusion.

"Wouldn't expect you here."

"I was just driving to pick up groceries for the double-wide."

"Don't you usually go to ShopRite?"

Lez's rudeness and confusion turned to defensive anger. By this point, she was famous for saying she only went to ShopRite because the smaller stores were too expensive. My grandmother was paying Lez and Rudge an obscene amount of money to do their jobs and the amount somehow leaked to many people in the area. I was surprised Mr. Grutt didn't know about it, let alone know Geneva had quit. Unless Mr. Grutt was playing ignorant, which, I must admit, was a deceitful ability a lot of people had up here. It was a form of politeness that had gone bad, as my grandmother put it.

"It's teeming with Hasidic Jews today," Lez defended. "I feel they may not be that clean and if I come back to my poor Rudge with a virus... that would just be the end of him. He's so tired, Jeanne. His back. His legs. I worry about his heart."

She said this because she had an audience with Mr. Grutt there. This was her time to build her image in the town: the perception of a hardworking couple being overworked by a lazy landowner. And she even tried to get the bonus point too by mentioning the Hasidic Jews. This would generate comradery with the locals, despite the fact she thought the town was antisemitic and had made that very clear to my grandmother one drunken night.

"His heart?" my grandmother asked, genuinely concerned. "You never told me anything about his heart."

"He's fine. I just worry about it. That kind of physical labor can give anyone a heart attack."

In the span of two months, Rudge had changed the knobs of three different doors in the house. He'd weed-whacked around the pool and then had to stop for three weeks because he threw out his back. Since then, not much else had been done around the property besides Lez coming in and out of the house saying how she didn't have enough time in the day to get everything done.

"Is he home?" my grandmother asked, looking outside to make sure he was.

"Yes. He's resting."

"Make sure he rests and takes all the time he needs."

"I've already told him that. Thank you."

"Is that . . ." my grandmother questioned, "Is that the red car out there?"

Lez went ghost white and then went tomato red. I had never seen that fluctuation in a person before.

"Yes," she said.

My grandmother waited for her to continue her response. This was a dangerous place for Lez to be in because for the first time my grandmother wouldn't be able to lie to herself about the truth of Lez. This was flagrant. Caught right in the act.

"I was planning on picking up groceries for the house," she said.

"Lez," my grandmother said, finding in herself a new sense of strength. "I told you that you could only use the red car for very specific and necessary outings. The insurance only covers that. If you get in an accident—"

"I could be hurt," she continued my grandmother's thought.

The truth was Lez was using the red car for everything. Gas prices were going up and she didn't want to pay for it. To her, my grandmother was a bank, and poor Lez was a charity that deserved every penny. There was truly a belief that she and Rudge should not be forced to pay for anything. If they paid, it was a form of abuse.

They were victims of the system even though they were playing that system. During work hours, my grandmother had Lez use the red car to do very specific errands. She rarely had Lez do this so, in theory, she should only use that car at most two or three times a month. My grandmother would leave the property much more now since she had full-time help. That meant it was only me in the house, which meant Lez could do just about anything she wanted. She would grab the key for the car and do it right in front of me. "I have to run to the dump," she'd say. "We recycle at the double-wide." Then she would walk past me in her entitled way and tie up the garbage in the kitchen with the bottles in it. She'd swing the bag over her shoulder like Santa Claus with his bag of toys. But, unlike Santa Claus, she would complain about it and act as if she were lugging a pile of bricks my grandmother subjected her to in this hellish servitude. "This is what's destroying the environment," she'd say, walking past me again. "We don't use bottles in the double-wide. Don't have the money to even if we wanted." Then she'd push the front door open and throw the bags in the trunk of the car and disappear for hours. The recycling center was at most a five-minute drive. But she was gone for hours. And my grandmother would get these large gas bills from her, and she'd do nothing about it. All the while, Lez's precious yellow Beetle was tucked away securely in the garage. It never left that garage because of a hailstorm we had once. My grandmother was out that day and Lez had run out of her house in a panic with a metal muffin tray over her head. You could hear the hail pinging off the muffin tray and Lez screaming with that high-pitched screeching voice of hers that didn't really sound human.

"Osk," she screamed. "Open the fucking garage. Torrance is getting pulverized out here. My poor Torrance. He's been through so much—a hundred and seventy-three thousand miles!"

I scrambled to get the remote key and she screamed at me some more. She made me feel like the stupid kid I was, and it set off my nerves and I couldn't think straight and my hands were shaking. I began to cry. She really was emotionally abusive. Horrible. Especially when my grandmother wasn't around.

The key finally worked, and the garage door opened very slowly. Lez missed the door by less than an inch as she raced in, and I wasn't sure she'd be able to stop in time before hitting the back wall of the garage. But she did. Her car must've had good brakes. Then she clicked the inside button and the door shut slowly. She wouldn't ask me to shut the door because I was an idiot to her. Minimal tasks for Osk because he'd surely screw them up.

Later that day, my grandmother pulled into the driveway and asked me if Lez had left as she walked over to the back door. It was amazing how no one ever asked about Rudge. He was never around. And when I say never, I mean never. I think he was one of those introverted homebodies. At night, I would see the lights of their TV blaring through their bedroom window like Times Square. But then the next day Lez would talk about how she never had time to watch movies or television. My grandmother would mention a new movie she saw, and Lez would give her the same answer every time.

"Rudge and I just don't have any time to watch movies," she'd say as she watered the plants. The only thing she did was water the plants. That would happen between four and five o'clock each afternoon for a maximum of twenty minutes. Then she would disappear to her house and consider work on her house to be work on the property. I guess it technically was. And Lez ran her life on technicalities. There was no passion in anything she did. It was all timed and calculated with her. Because she really hated us. She hated country people. This was an experience for her, and we happened to be the vermin in her pretty rural narrative. Funny how people who really hated people seemed to have the most opinions on how other people should be treated. It was always the quiet ones who really cared. Those unseen heroes were doing all the good behind the scenes. My grandmother was one of them and Lez knew it and hated her even more for it. And it would be her sole mission to take control of perception, which my grandmother was terrible at, and make it seem as if my grandmother was really the villain. She was attempting to achieve this at the Grutt-Kutt gas station.

"I know," Lez responded to my grandmother in a frantic high-pitched voice. "Jeanne, I took the red car because that road you have is very rough on cars . . . unfairly tough . . ."

My grandmother waited for a better response before she shut her down. People of her generation maintained a sense of honor even when their adversary lacked any trace of it. Roles switched, Lez would've made a massacre of my grandmother if she'd had the upper hand. There was a ruthless hatred fused into the building blocks of moral superiority with people today. Lez taught me that very well. She taught me a lot about that other very public face of society.

"Okay," Lez sighed. "Guess it will be ruined."

"What?" my grandmother asked.

"Well . . ."

"What?"

"It's your birthday tomorrow, right?"

"Yes, Lez."

"Rudge sent me over here to buy you a cake."

Silence. Mr. Grutt seemed disappointed in my grandmother and my grandmother seemed disappointed in herself. I was confused. I didn't know if I should believe her. She was that good. Even the child who had seen everything didn't know if she was still scheming. She could trick a fly on the wall.

"Oh, Lez," my grandmother said with her head down. "I'm so sorry. That's so sweet of you and Rudge. I guess . . . you see . . . we just never celebrate birthdays around here . . . so . . . I—well, I guess we just forget. Thank you for remembering."

Lez could dig in now because that's what she did. Ruthless.

"Rudge even has your birthday marked in the calendar on the fridge. A big heart around 'Jeanne's B-Day!!!'"

She made sure to mention the three exclamation points. Jerk.

"Oh, Lez," my grandmother could only say. That was all she had left in her.

"We scraped together some money to pay for it. I know it's expensive here, but Rudge and I wanted to make it special. We couldn't go to ShopRite for Jeanne's birthday. I hear they have great ice-cream cakes here. Isn't ice-cream cake your favorite?"

"Oh, Lez."

Mr. Grutt's leathered wet-cigar-skinned face drooped in complete disappointment of my grandmother. Because she was now the new symbol of oppression to this struggling store owner in a small town. You may as well be put to death if you find yourself in that position here. And Lez had achieved a multipronged attack. She knew how involved Mr. Grutt was in the affairs of the community and she knew this altercation may as well have been the splashed lead story in the local newspaper. Check. She also established herself as the victim. A poor underpaid woman who was using her own money to do something nice for her employer. Why wouldn't she use the property owner's car to get a gift for her? Check. Now, for the real, irreparable damage. In Mr. Grutt's eyes, my grandmother was now the difficult employer, and this opened those wounds harkening back to his old employer who had once fired him, leaving him stranded without any health benefits. Check. Done. Success. Tarred and feathered.

"Do you still want the cake?" Lez asked as the last twist of the blade.

My grandmother couldn't put the words together. Her embarrassment had crystallized into shock.

"Jeanne loves our ice-cream cakes," Mr. Grutt said, like my grandmother was some royal pig.

"Let them eat cake," Lez said under her breath. She stiffly scurried over to the ice-cream cakes because the store clearly grossed her out. Too much humanity, I assumed she thought. Picking a cake fast, she scurried over to the counter and pushed my Hostess pile aside.

"Ewwww," she said, eyeing the HoHos. She fingered at it like it was a dirty diaper. "Guess someone wants cancer tomorrow," she hissed.

Mr. Grutt laughed because Lez was on his good side. If she had said this before the incident, he would've taken deep offense to that.

"You don't like HoHos?" he asked.

"Not if I want to make it to my next birthday," she said like a teenage girl.

He laughed again. She had him. And he thought she was pretty, so she really had him. My grandmother was the scum of the town now. He wouldn't even really look at her. That rich oppressor. A slaveowner. The kryptonite to red-blooded blue-collar struggling self-employed gas station owners.

The bell rang again, and the door screamed like Lez.

"Lez," a familiar voice said. "What's taking so long? I want to get to the outlets. Oh my God, this is straight out of a Cormac McCarthy novel!"

It was the owl. He floated in and stopped dead in his tracks when he realized my grandmother was there. He couldn't care less about me—the mute child. "Oh," he said and covered his mouth in a surprised but delicate way. "I'll get back to the car then."

The blood drained from Lez's face again and Mr. Grutt made eye contact with my grandmother. He was the judge and he wanted to see my grandmother's next move. This could be her chance.

But it wasn't.

My grandmother folded. Because she needed Lez. Or at least she thought she did.

"Go have fun at the outlets," she abdicated. "And thank you for thinking of me. I'm glad someone does."

Mr. Grutt looked down at the counter and rang up the ice-cream cake and put it into one of those big cold plastic bags. Lez grabbed the bag and whisked by me. She had a way of blowing around the air as she passed you. It was like her own little storm. This time that air was the only communication my grandmother would get, and she would take it, defeated.

"Jeanne," Mr. Grutt said without looking at her. "I'll ring you up?"

"Yes, Max," she answered, stepping up to the counter like someone stepping up to the noose.

"If they go to the outlets," Mr. Grutt commented, "that ice-cream cake is going to melt in the car."

My grandmother agreed through her silence. She paid for the groceries, and I followed her out to the car. The HoHos weren't as good as they normally were that day. In fact, that was the last time I ever bought them.

◆

As the years went by, I randomly developed an obsession for kart racing and I saved up my money to buy my first go-kart, which was equipped with a 196 cc, 9 hp, 4-stroke automatic engine. It revved to 3,600 rpm and hit about 35 mph. My grandmother felt awful I had to use my life savings for this off-roading marvel of engineering, but she could do nothing about it because her money was locked up so tightly with Lez and Rudge. It was all going to them, and Lez somehow negotiated a yearly 10 percent increase in salary due to inflation. That would make sense if Lez and Rudge had actual expenses. But, as of that time, they had no house to pay for and their car was permanently stowed away in the garage. Eleven months went by without them taking their car out. And Lez could get away with this because she had made my grandmother feel so guilty about the quality of the roads around the property. As a consequence, my grandmother gave her a free pass to use the red car as much as she wanted. I could drive now, and my grandmother had been hoping to give me that red car, but now she couldn't because Lez needed it. And I couldn't use my grandmother's car because she had the driver's seat customized to cater to her growing back problems. Her seat was locked in place now, without the ability to move it backward or forward. And since I was growing an average of five inches a year, the time had passed for me long before to be able to use her car. She felt mortified by the fact the money was gone. So I guess my love for karting came at a perfect time.

My go-kart was my first car, really. And I didn't care. But it was so embarrassing for my grandmother. It was fine, though, to me. I would sometimes take my go-kart out to town because Lez would go off somewhere with the red car for hours, which meant I couldn't share it even if I wanted to. But I didn't. I would never share anything with her. And she wouldn't share anything with me. I remember once when I had to move the red car out of the driveway because my grandmother was too nervous to bother Lez at her house that day. Lez was on my grandmother's time when this happened, but my grandmother was still too shy to bother her. Having Lez move the red car out of the driveway each time she did this and pull it back in each time was too much of an ask for someone like Lez. And Lez knew my grandmother's schedule and would still park right behind her on those days because parking on the grass near the barn was, as she would always say, "bad for Torrance's poor tires." Torrance was her baby, but she would always leave the keys in the front dish of our house to remind us that Torrance's upkeep was still my grandmother's responsibility. It was a funny passive-aggressive gesture of not claiming ownership because my grandmother had already spent thousands on Lez's accidents and Lez still refused to leave the car over at the barn because the moisture of the grass supposedly deteriorated the rubber of the tires. I guess frontal impact into a tree due to alcohol consumption was better for a car. Somehow my grandmother had gotten her out of that one, twice. Good thing my grandmother was friends with the sheriff. But there was nothing she could do about her insurance going through the roof. That, she couldn't get out of. Money was money. Premiums were premiums. And losing money was losing money. My grandmother had only one option for this: denial. And this denial became eerily clear the morning her accountant came over for coffee.

"Jeanne, you can't do this anymore," he said to her, cupping the hot coffee in his hands.

"Bacon?" my grandmother asked.

"Jeanne."

"Yes, George, I hear you."

"I don't think you do, Jeanne."

"Trust me, I do."

"Something has to give."

"I know."

"And you can't give anymore."

"I know."

"Do you?"

"It was so different with Arnold and Geneva."

"Very different."

"Simpler, you know. People's lives are so much more complicated now."

"How do you mean, Jeanne?"

"Lez and Rudge. They have complicated lives."

"How does this affect you?"

"I know I'm paying them too much, George."

"Grossly, Jeanne."

"Who else is going to do the work? You?"

"No. I'm your accountant."

"I need them, George."

"I understand. But they need to understand they need you too."

"They do."

"They don't, Jeanne."

"What do you suppose I do then?"

"What I would do, or what you would do?"

"George, I know what you would do."

"This 'sweat equity' is a load of—"

"Please, George."

"Fine. I understand you've worked out a substitution for rent. But that isn't going to cut it."

"I can't suddenly ask—"

"Yes, you can. Financial situations are always in flux. Things change for me when they change for my boss. It's how this thing goes. Don't you see? Where do you think the money is coming from? They think of you as Bank of America, Jeanne."

My grandmother began to cry, and George had never seen this before. He was stunned and didn't know how to react. He would look at me in desperation. And I would have nothing to offer.

"Jeanne," he said and leaned over the table, nearly spilling his coffee.

"Sorry," he went on as he caught the coffee.

"George. George. You're right. I know you're right. Everyone knows you're right. The ghosts of my ancestors in this darn house know you're right."

George smiled and sat back in his chair. He would make sure no coffee got on his tie. It didn't.

"As I said," George said, "something has to give. You need to ask them to pay rent. Or you must cut their salary. What does Rudge do here?"

At first, my grandmother couldn't answer. At second, she couldn't answer, either. "Rudge?" she punted.

"Yes, Rudge."

"He..."

Silence.

"He..."

Silence.

"Rudge..."

"Jeanne?"

"He's been having a tough time, George."

"And so have you. It isn't all about them."

"I know."

"You keep saying that."

"I know," she repeated and laughed.

"I suspect you'll choose the rent route...?"

"I suppose."

"I can't see you cutting their salary."

"It seems so wrong to do that."

George pulled out a sheet of paper and a pen. He wrote something down on this sheet of paper and slid it over to my grandmother across the table.

"No," my grandmother said and pushed it back to him.

"No?"

"Can't do that."

"Why?"

"They would never do that."

"It isn't a matter of choice, Jeanne."

"How can I go from not having them pay anything to paying that?"

"You shouldn't have done what you did in the first place."

"That isn't fair, George."

"It's not about what's fair. This is serious stuff, Jeanne. This is your financial future. You can't be selling stock the way you've been."

"What the hell is the point of having it then?"

"For it to grow."

"I'm not growing. I'm just getting older. And this property is getting older, and we need someone here to take care of it."

"Arnold did a wonderful job and he never lived here. This couple lives here and I haven't seen the furniture taken out to the pool or the back terrace once this summer—or last summer for that matter."

"Rudge has back problems. And it's a lot to take out of the barn. Those are metal chairs and tables."

"How did Arnold do it?"

"I don't know how Arnold did it. As I said, George, this new generation is a lot more complicated. Arnold was simpler."

It was so odd. My grandmother was almost complaining about Arnold because he had done his job right. This was purely defensive since the comparison of Arnold to Lez and Rudge was sickening. George would always bring this up to draw blood.

"The property isn't any more complicated, Jeanne," George said, now grabbing my grandmother's hands from across the table. I think he thought he was finally getting through to her. "Jeanne," he went on, miving his chair next to hers. "You're going to lose this place. It'll all be dried up—all of it—in less than a year if you keep going at this rate."

My grandmother cried into George's shoulder and George held her and let her cry it out.

"Fine," she finally said. "I'll talk to them."

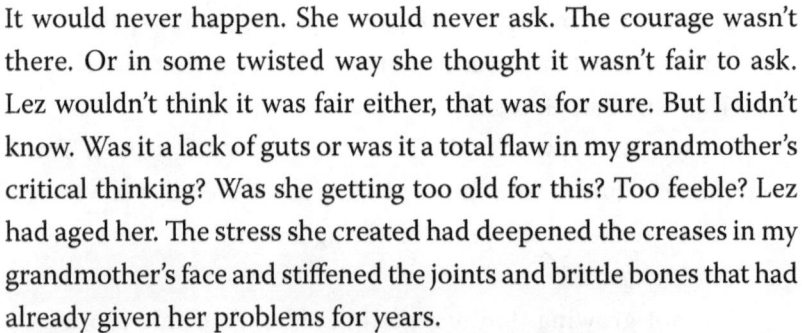

It would never happen. She would never ask. The courage wasn't there. Or in some twisted way she thought it wasn't fair to ask. Lez wouldn't think it was fair either, that was for sure. But I didn't know. Was it a lack of guts or was it a total flaw in my grandmother's critical thinking? Was she getting too old for this? Too feeble? Lez had aged her. The stress she created had deepened the creases in my grandmother's face and stiffened the joints and brittle bones that had already given her problems for years.

George wasn't invited over anymore, and I didn't know the reasoning for this either. Whether she couldn't see him out of shame or disagreement, it was impossible for me to tell. There was something very unfriendly about my grandmother now, and she hid her relationship with these caretakers like a teenager would hide her bad boyfriend relations from her parents. Everyone was a form of parental guidance around her, even though she was most likely the oldest one in the room. People had opinions because they cared about her and wanted the property to succeed. George came out with alternative caretaking options. He didn't have to do that, but he wanted to. He would risk his business relationship with my grandmother because he cared about her enough to do so. The community still loved her. She was an institution to them. But she was just a stack of money dwindling in height each day to Lez and Rudge, and Lez would not let go of her until there was nothing left to take. It wasn't just the money they were sucking away. The Jeanne everyone knew was disappearing.

"Let's watch a movie, Osk," my grandmother said to me about eight months after she told George she'd ask Lez and Rudge for rent.

"Sure," I said. "What type?"

The movies my grandmother would watch with me were very limited but now that I was older, I was hoping the range would open.

"How about *The Godfather*?"

"*The Godfather*?" I asked, not believing I had finally reached the required age.

"Yes. You've always wanted to see that movie."

"I have. I—"

"Let's put it on, then."

I grabbed the VHS, slipped the hunk of plastic out of the box, ejected another VHS that had probably been in there for years, and pushed *The Godfather* into the TV. It's small screen sat nestled in an enormous cabinet console.

"Easy now, Osk," she laughed. "You don't want to jam it."

"We'll have to watch all the other ones, too," I said, frantic with excitement.

"One at a time. You have to watch this one first."

This was my way of asking if I could watch all three and this was her way of saying I could. My heart was fluttering. *The Godfather* trilogy. The greatest trilogy of all time. *The Lord of the Rings* was close—a close second, I assumed I would think. And that turned out to be true after I completed *The Godfather* trilogy. It wouldn't have been so close if the third one hadn't been so bad. It wasn't misunderstood, as some fans said. It was bad, I thought. But the first one was just so good. And it was hard watching it with my grandmother there because Vito Corleone reminded me of her. The way he was in the beginning. That wedding scene. The way people came in and out of his office asking for favors and giving respect—that is how my grandmother had been. She was the godfather of her town and this property. She would do anything for anybody, and they would do anything for her. There was always a balance. Always giving back on both ends for the favors that were selflessly handed out. That balance. I missed that. And my grandmother did, too. Because it kept her strong. She could be a good person without selling herself. A return on investment was guaranteed. No contract. No shake of the hand. It was understood that balance would be struck no matter what. My grandmother was the foundation on which this whole system worked and, as the movie went on, I could see more and more of this used-up property owner's age coming through her formerly upbeat and youthful persona. The ending of that movie was her now. The heart attack in the garden while playing with his grandson. Frail Vito. That is what my grandmother had become. Not the confident alpha quietly requiring respect with subordinates he considered family. I wondered if that's how my grandmother would go. I wondered.

The Godfather became my favorite movie of all time. It's no question the greatest movie ever made, and my grandmother laughed when I told her that.

"There's so many more movies to see," she said to me. My grandmother loved film and she had a stack of VHSs in the living room behind the piano. Most of them she hadn't let me watch before, but now, finally, I was of age. It wasn't just me looking at the VHS covers, imagining what the movie was like.

"Like what?" I asked.

"Oh, wow. That's a question. So many, Osk. You have *Citizen Kane*. You have *Taxi Driver*. Ahhh, you have *Raging Bull*. You have *There Will Be Blood*. So many. *2001: A Space Odyssey*. Too many to list, Osk. *The Shining*. So many. *Barry Lyndon*. The beauty of *Eyes Wide Shut*—not the storyline. I can go on and on."

"I want to see all those movies."

"We can. We should start with the old ones first. All on VHS. There Will Be Blood and Eyes Wide Shut I have DVDs for."

"Okay."

It was getting darker out and the high beams of a car came through the windows and scorched our eyes. It scanned by our retinas slowly and we both covered our faces and ducked like this was some alien invasion.

"What in the name," my grandmother said, rising from the couch and shuffling her way to the front door.

"Who is it?" I asked, concerned, thinking this was an extraterrestrial experience. The quiet of the country could get a young boy thinking very off into the unknown when something irregular happened.

"Rudge," my grandmother called. "Is that you?"

"Yes, Jeanne," Rudge answered. "It's me. Sorry to bother you."

"Oh, no worries. Whose car is that?"

Lez and Rudge always drove with the high beams on, and Rudge took his time parking the car very carefully in the driveway before he took a moment to answer my grandmother. He also inspected the outside of the car, knowing my grandmother was standing there waiting for him to respond.

"My car," he answered. "Got it today."

"A new car?"

My grandmother nearly fell backward because Lez had convinced her to cover her insurance costs. She told my grandmother that Rudge had been demoted and was awaiting termination any day now. Oh, I forgot to tell this part of the story. Due to Rudge's health, Lez demanded he get another job so they both had proper insurance. This was something my grandmother could not do for some reason. But I was still confused about why my grandmother was paying for Lez's insurance if she was covered by Rudge's. The whole thing made no sense, and my grandmother was very sketchy about it. I never asked because I was just a kid. I found everything out by spying. And this I couldn't piece together.

"Is that a Cadillac?" my grandmother probed.

"A Caddy it is."

Rudge had no shame. He knew why my grandmother was asking.

"Nice car," she said.

"It is."

"Used?"

"Nope. Newer than new."

"How's that job holding up?"

"Playing it day-by-day."

"You know, I wanted to get Osk a car."

"Oh, is that right?"

"Yes."

"Well," he said and slapped his legs to get himself moving. "I better get back to the double-wide."

Lez had trained him to say that very well.

"Better get inside," my grandmother said. "Think a storm's coming."

"A storm?"

"Yes, didn't you put the radio on?"

Rudge ran back to his car and snapped at my grandmother to open the garage with the remote. My grandmother was old and that would mean she'd have to run to the back of the house where the remote was.

"I'll get it," I said to my grandmother, disappointed in her weakness.

"Thank you, Osk," she said, wounded and feeble.

Rudge screamed "Fuck" as the garage door opened to reveal the yellow Beetle.

"Fucking Lez," he yelled and hopped up and down on the ground. For someone with such physical problems, he sure hopped up and down well.

He floored the car backward and ripped up the grass as he swerved around my grandmother's car to get to the barn. The car came to a halt and the driver's door swung open and Rudge ran to the sliding barn doors and typed in the passcode to open the lock. After pulling the heavy barn doors open with aggressive, exhaling anger, he ran back to the car and slammed the driver's door shut. "Fuck," he said again and got out of the car. "The fucking lawnmower." He pulled the lawnmower out of the barn to make room for his new Cadillac and speed-walked back to his car with his hands swaying wildly, slashing at his hips. "Stupid lawnmower," he said one last time before shutting the driver's door. A brief pause. Then the brake lights flickered as he gently pulled the car into the barn. You could tell he really didn't want to hit anything, and you could tell he hated everything in that barn, even the lawnmower my grandmother had bought them to mow their own lawn. That lawnmower he left inside the barn, and it was my grandmother's old Simplicity lawnmower he took out. But he still hated his own lawnmower because it could harm his new car. There was no thought about this being my grandmother's barn in the first place. No, this was a building built solely to protect his precious Caddy. And my grandmother made it difficult for him to do that by having her own stuff in her own barn.

The brake lights stopped flickering and Rudge cut the engine and speed-walked to the barn doors and shut them with the same exhaling anger.

"Lez should've sent me a message," he said to my grandmother. "Half the time it's a hailstorm up here."

He didn't walk up the stairs of the front porch to say hello and instead went right past my grandmother to the house she'd built for him. There was no goodnight. Nothing. Just a complaint about Lez and some more cursing. My grandmother didn't know how to respond and sunk back into the depths of the house, silenced by her muted misery. Lez ran in, uninvited, and went to the TV where we watched *The Godfather*. She pried the VHS out of the TV in a state of madness and she saw it wasn't the right one.

"Where's . . . ?" she said, searching around the living room. "My tape. It was recording my show. The next episode. Where's my tape?"

My grandmother was too tired to respond to her and I helped her search for her tape. I was afraid it was the one I took out. And it was.

"You took it out?" she asked, in my face, after I handed her the tape. "When?"

"Just before. To watch a movie."

"*The Godfather*?" she asked, holding it and pointing it in my face. "Like you haven't seen this a thousand times."

"I haven't, actually."

"Christ, really?" she sighed. "All you privileged are so sheltered."

"I'm sorry."

"You should be. I was recording my show. Rudge and I don't have the money for cable, so we record cable shows on this TV. I told Jeanne this. Now we can't watch the show. We won't know what happens. And the episode after this will make no sense to us. The show is ruined."

"I thought you don't have time to watch TV," I said, innocently.

"Excuse me?"

"I thought that's what you said."

"Am I your slave, Osk?"

"No," I cried.

"Do I say 'yessum' like Geneva did?"

"What?"

"Do I say 'yessum' and 'Mr. Oscar' like Geneva?"

"I don't understand."

"You wouldn't," she said with some new Bronx accent she acquired for the purpose of putting me down. "You're all privileged."

Then she stalked out with her tape, and I didn't see my grandmother for the rest of the night. I'm sure she listened to that interaction and, as Lez stormed away, dissolved back into her bedroom, dreaming of the happy memories of this now hijacked house. Those happy dreams filling her old mind until sometime in the middle of the night when the worst hailstorm in decades came through and destroyed her car. The windshield was covered in cracks and the bodywork was showered with indentations. The front lights of the lawnmower were also cracked.

The next morning Lez was the first to discover the damage that'd been done, and she'd later that day tell my grandmother, "Thank God Rudge took out your Simplicity with its heavy, expensive metal. It can take a beating. Our cheap Husqvarna would've been pulverized. That would've been the end of Husky." She would not mention my grandmother's car because that required sympathy and sympathy was something Lez received and never gave. And I also noticed she never named the vehicles my grandmother owned.

Karting became my escape, and I got better and better at it. I built an off-road track that went through the property and friends came over with their karts to race. I would always win. My grandmother put me in constant competitions throughout the state and beyond, and I won basically all of them. I actually made quite a bit of money from it and, unfortunately, it was all used to support the property. My grandmother had weekly breakdowns because of this but there was no choice. My karting victories were helping us keep the place alive, especially with the added financial weight of Lez and Rudge. Then it got to the point where my winning streak propelled me to regional recognition. I won the New York Junior Kart Championship three years in a row and the possibility of Formula Three in the future was not so unreachable. Real fans came to watch me. It wasn't just parents anymore. People who I didn't know came to watch and it wasn't like their kids were also racing. They came to watch me—just me.

I had my first big accident when I did my first race out of state. The nerves settled in, and it tightened me and, consequently, the agility and handling of the kart. I hit a lamppost and was knocked out until I awoke to my grandmother tossing water on my face. People really did that. Seemed like something they only did in the movies. And I was watching a lot of movies now. And my grandmother gave me more responsibilities around the house and even the property. She let me drive her car, and I did everything for it. Its maintenance was my job. I serviced it myself. I tuned the engine. I changed the oil. Fixed the brakes. Everything. I knew that car better than anyone on this planet. Only once did my grandmother have to go to the mechanic. That time, Lez had convinced my grandmother it needed a little more than "kid's work." So, she took it to the mechanic, and I wasn't happy because they did what I would've done. It also cost my grandmother five hundred dollars. But the mechanic had become friends with Lez because he wanted to get into her pants. A lot of guys in the town were attracted to Lez. I didn't really understand it, but I guess she had a way with men. I was certainly immune to that. Thank God. She hated men she couldn't manipulate, so it made sense she disliked me so much.

I couldn't say the same for Tori. Her I fell for. Hard. And she was beautiful. Perfect, really. I met her at a race. Her father was a fan of mine and he followed me throughout New York State. He watched all three of my championship wins. My second win I broke the lap record, which hadn't been broken in five years. But it wasn't just about that. It was about how I broke it. The previous record was obliterated, and many thought my new record would never be topped again. Not to sound like a jerk, but I agreed with them. I never voiced it, but I agreed with them. And my grandmother made sure I kept my ego in check. I was hyperfocused and sometimes I came off like something I really wasn't. My developmental pediatrician had told my grandmother when I was younger that I was on the "spectrum." I didn't know what that meant, and my grandmother wasn't the greatest at describing it to me. I had put together that it meant I was a little different. That's all I knew. And when I would do odd things, I'd think to myself, *That's the spectrum behavior.* And it turned off a lot of people. But not Tori. It turned off her dad when he finally met me. I can't remember what I said but it resulted in him no longer going to any of my races. After I first met Tori at that race, she had her mother bring her. Tori told me her father still asked her for the results when she got home. It was always me winning. I guess I am a little cocky. A bit of a jerk. But I didn't mean to be. I really didn't.

My life was racing and Tori. And the fact they could happen at the same time made my life idyllic. To see Tori right there at the finish. The fans behind her and seeing that smile on her face. I have trouble describing how she looked because it was so personal to me. Blond hair. Blue eyes. Fair skin. Petite. That sort of thing, I guess. But I told her everything. She knew more about me than my grandmother did, and she told me everything about herself. I knew from her that her mother was a very good woman. And her father was a very competitive and devoted dad. Tori wasn't an athlete, although she did snowboard on a recreational level. There was no possibility of her going pro snowboarding like I was with my racing.

When I began to win regionally, that's when career-makers came to watch me. Tori's father came around to liking me after I spent many dinners at their place, and he would watch the bigger races. He even flew to a few of them and brought Tori with him. I won those, too, and made the news a few times. It was known publicly that Tori was my girlfriend, and it took some getting used to for her father. But he loved the attention and really became a good father figure to me. He was very devoted, and I envied the devotion Tori'd had all her life without even realizing. Even when I was winning races, I still envied this devotion. I had a level of it from my grandmother, but she was too tired at this point to really give me what I needed, especially through the awkward years, which I was living through now. But I got the attention I needed from Tori's parents, and in my weird and random way one night, I asked them to become my parents. It was at dinner and Tori nearly spit out her food.

"We're flattered," Tori's mom answered, not knowing what else to say.

"How would your parents feel about that?" Tori's dad continued for her.

"My dad is dead, and my mom is in rehab, now... at least I think so. She's been gone most of my life."

And there it was. That's how Tori's parents found out about my sad life. I guess this is how you find out too. Tori already knew. I told her everything. I refused to hold anything back from her, no matter what it was. I needed someone like Tori in my life. Someone who could be my object of total trust and transparency. It used to be my grandmother, but she had become a shell of herself. Lez had sucked the life out of her like you'd suck the marrow out of a bone. She'd become a little bland to talk to about important stuff. Sad. But true.

"I'm so sorry," Tori's mom said and put her silverware down. "Do you want to talk about it, Oscar?"

"Not much to really say," I dove in. "My dad was blown up overseas. And my mom got into drugs and dated her drug dealer."

"Your father was blown up overseas?" Tori's mom asked, so concerned.

"Roadside bomb."

"How terrible."

"My mom couldn't take it, so she left me with my grandmother—temporarily, at first. She then traveled a bit and then came back and met some drug addict at a bar in Buffalo. Don't know why she was up there. But she was. And they started to date, and he got my mom into some bad drugs. She got HIV from him."

Tori's dad dropped his knife against the plate. A dollop of mashed potato flung onto the table mat, and he scrambled to clean it up.

"HIV?" he asked.

"Yeah, I found out about that from my grandmother. She doesn't let my mother come by anymore. One time my mother tried to come, and my grandmother took me out the whole day in anticipation of her arrival. The caretakers said they never saw her. My mom always says she's going to do things and never follows through. My grandmother knows that. But she was so serious about her not seeing me that she still took me out on the very off chance my mother came to see me. I was even taken to this therapist for some time. It timed out, though—the therapy. But when I had it, I had to go. I talked to the woman about my mom... and the HIV... and the drugs. She asked how I felt about all of this. I told her about this fantasy I had. Slitting my wrists watching a classic eighties movie. Dying watching an eighties movie—how twisted is that, right? I can never remember exactly what the movie was in this crazy fantasy of mine. I guess it's like Adventures in Babysitting or something like that. I don't even know why I'm thinking of that movie—first to come to mind, I guess... who knows. Anyway, we got into a few other things, too. Like, uhhh, what was it? Oh, yes. We talked about this 'obsession' I had with *It's a Wonderful Life*—the movie, you know. The therapist was really into it. Why this movie? We would always come back to this movie even if we weren't talking about it. I told her I guess I thought I was George Bailey or something like that. She asked why. Each time. Like I would give her a different answer or something. Must've been a logic to it. So, I told her, each time, it was because I felt trapped. I don't really know why. But that was my answer. Maybe there's something to it. Because George Bailey felt trapped in that town, Bedford Falls. She thought the house and the property was my Bedford Falls. That was her conclusion. She thought I really didn't like it—hated it... actually. But I don't think so. How could I hate it up here? I think she was wrong. I don't hate it here."

"Is she still with that man?" Tori's mom asked, brushing aside the bizarreness of my suicidal fantasy and the oddity of my George Bailey likeness.

"I don't know, actually. We don't really talk much about her these days."

"I can see why not," Tori's dad commented.

"Carl," Tori's mom said and slapped his shoulder. I know he didn't mean it in a bad way.

"It's fine," I said. "I don't like talking about her."

Tori rubbed my back and changed the subject. She was so mature for her age, and she had such good parents.

"Formula Three is right around the corner—no pun intended," she said and cut firmly into the turkey, making that fine scratching sound on the plate. I hated that scratching sound.

"It is," her dad said. "It'll be a different level."

"Yeah, Dad, but he's got this."

"Oh, he definitely does. Then off to Formula One. How about Formula One?"

I laughed.

"How about it?" he asked again.

"Those aren't go-karts," I answered. "I spend half my time driving around on a dirt course I built with a throw-around off-road go-kart my grandmother gave me. It's great. But it goes thirty-five miles an hour."

"That's for fun. The shifter karts you race are different."

"Yeah, I mean—"

"Come on."

"Totally different—yeah. But it's not . . . I would have to be—"

"I could see you doing damage in Formula One."

"Right now, I have my eyes set on the CRG Road Rebel Shifter Kart. That's where I am right now. I could do damage with that."

"Is that the one with the Honda CR125 Stock Engine?"

"Yes. And the MyChron 4 Basic data system."

"Thirty-two millimeter chassis?"

"Yessir. Six-speed. Magnesium wheels. Fiberglass seats. Steel brakes."

"Heavens. What about the Intrepid Cruiser Shifter Kart?"

In total amusement, Tori and her mom watched us talk back and forth, digging each other deeper into this go-kart talk.

"Aluminum frame?" I asked, knowing I was right.

"Indeed," he answered, knowing I would be right.

"Six-speed also. I like the one with the Honda CR250cc shifter engine."

"Vortex ROK Shifter?"

"I also like that."

"Super Shifter?"

"Yup. You can't go wrong with the Super Shifter."

"How about the Daymak C5 Blast?"

"Really?"

"Yeah."

"Have you seen one?"

"No."

"Me neither."

"You should drive one," he baited.

"That's scary fast."

"You could tear apart the track with that."

"And kill myself," I said. "Ten thousand watt motor. An output of ninety-six kg of upward thrust. The thing is electric. Sixty kg of forward thrust from four rear EDF motors."

"What's the zero to sixty?"

"one point five seconds."

"No, come on."

"I'm serious," I laughed. "One point five seconds."

"Faster than any Ferrari."

"No question."

"Jesus."

"About eighty grand."

"For a go-kart?"

"For a go-kart. It isn't cheap to go zero to sixty in one-point-five seconds."

"Good deal when you compare it to a Ferrari."

"Guess you could look at it that way," I said and made eye contact with Tori to thank her for listening to us so patiently. She smiled. I really did love her.

"What do you race with now?" he asked, winding down the conversation. Tori's mom was starting to lose patience.

"An old Rotax. Got it from one of the guys for nothing."

"All the more to you. That's why Formula Three is right around the corner, if you can do what you do with an old Rotax. Tori's going to have to follow you around all over the world soon enough."

Tori kissed me and then held my hand under the table.

"All over Europe," she said, "and even Japan."

I laughed again.

"Don't be so surprised when it happens, Oscar," he said, very seriously, like a father would. "You have that racing blood. It's in your eyes. The focus. The commitment. The will to win. It's in those eyes of yours. I saw it from the beginning when I first started to watch you race."

Tori had the family I never had. That support was something I hadn't known. It's something a grandmother can't give you. There had to be a real family structure for that to happen, and Tori had it. She had been loved so much and she had so much love to give. I was lucky I was on the receiving end of that. It almost made up for my upbringing. Almost.

◆

Tori's family moved to Munster, Indiana, and Tori would fly in every other month to visit me for an extended weekend. I was sad to see them leave but I was used to the disappointment, so the blow was cushioned a bit by experience.

"Working on the car again?" Tori asked right when she arrived. I was tinkering with my grandmother's car, doing an oil change. Tori loved watching me do those things. She said it gave her a "brain massage" to watch me do boring work. She was a little strange and I loved her for it.

"Oil change," I said, giving her a kiss.

"Dropping the bags at the house."

"Okay."

"Any lunch?"

"Inside. Chicken salad at the table."

"Hope Ernie doesn't get it."

"He's outside. I let him out this morning."

"Deep in the woods, as always."

"We need to get him this time," I said. "Before it gets dark."

"Coyotes?"

"Yes. You can hear them yapping along the stream. My grandmother was freaked that one night we couldn't find him. She heard that yapping and nearly cried."

"I don't like those woods."

"Me neither."

"Okay. Going in. Be back in a sec."

"All right."

I continued changing the oil and I played "He Stopped Loving Her Today" from a small speaker I had. I missed Geneva and the song made me think of her and the way the house used to be. My grandmother couldn't bear to hear it and wouldn't come out when I played it. She understood I had to play it, and I made sure not to play it too much.

On the ground on a cloth, I had my equipment organized. I had the oil filter. I had the socket wrench. The oil filter wrench. The funnel. The oil pan and tons of rags and newspapers. I would then first drain the old motor oil. To do this, I put some newspapers out with the oil pan on them. I used the socket wrench to twist open the drain plug. You always turn the drain plug counterclockwise and, once it's done draining, you put the plug back on in a clockwise motion. After you do that, you replace the oil filter by loosening it with the filter wrench and by putting motor oil on the new gasket. You don't want the gasket to crack, which will result in an oil leak. That's why you put motor oil on the gasket. Then you add the new motor oil, and you loosen the cap and you put the motor oil into the tank very carefully. A funnel will help you with this. Then make sure to replace the cap and let your engine run for a few minutes to get the oil moving. Before you're done, see what the oil level is one last time with the dipstick. Then you're done. And too bad I was done right before Tori got back.

"You're done?" she asked.

"Yup."

"What the hell, Osk."

"What?" I asked, wiping my hands with the rags.

"You know I love watching."

"It's just an oil change."

"That's my favorite thing to watch."

"Should've been a little quicker."

"Damn."

"You can watch me put the stuff away."

"There's no fun in that."

"And there's fun in watching me do an oil change?"

"Yes."

"You're an odd one."

"And you . . . ?"

"I didn't say I wasn't odd."

"Everyone thinks you're odd."

"You haven't met 'everyone.'"

"Osk, I could only assume."

"Everyone thinks you're hot."

"No!"

"Yes."

"How?"

"Look at you."

"Me?"

"No, me. Yes, you."

"Easy on the eye, I guess."

"You are."

"You are too, Osk."

"Not really."

"I mean, you do have a strange smile," she laughed. "Where did you get that smile?"

"Not from my mother."

"Your father?"

"I can't really remember."

"I bet he had a good, traditional smile. I'm sure it's from your grandfather."

"Why don't you ask my grandmother."

"I can't ask her."

"Why not?"

"Because I can't ask your grandmother if her late husband had a strange smile."

"She would think it was funny."

"No, she would think it was offensive."

"It's hard to offend her."

Lez appeared. She was always appearing but not really doing anything. Tori didn't like her, and Lez could smell the dislike.

"She's so creepy," Tori whispered.

"They seem to be everywhere but nowhere."

"I know."

"Hey, can you help me bring this stuff into the garage?" Lez asked.

"It's covered in crap," I replied.

"Please."

"All right. Fine."

We went into the garage and Lez watched us to make sure we didn't scuff her car squeezing by it to get into my workshop room. My workshop room was in the back of the garage, and we had to shuffle our bodies between the shelves along the sides and Lez's annoying car.

"Watch your zippers," Lez would always say. And she also said it this time. Tori rolled her eyes.

"Does she think she owns this place?" Tori asked.

"I don't know."

"Really. She's extremely annoying."

"I know. I know."

"And your grandmother doesn't just give it to her?"

"I don't know, Tori."

Whenever I put her name in the answer, she knew that meant I didn't want to talk about it anymore. I did it this way because I didn't want to tell her to shut up.

We placed the equipment in a wooden box I'd built and squeezed out of the garage to look for Ernie.

"We can't just call him," Tori said after we'd both practically lost our voices from shouting. "Let's search."

"All right. Not too far, though."

"Wait," she said, stopping me with her arm against my chest.

"What?"

"Hear that?"

"No."

"Listen. Listen."

I listened. Nothing.

"You don't hear that?" she asked.

"No."

"It sounds like a person."

"A person?"

"Calling us. You really can't hear that?"

I listened again. Nothing.

"Come," she said and dragged me into the woods.

"Tori, what's wrong with you?"

"Come."

"Tori."

"Please, Osk. Just come."

"All right."

I followed right behind her, and we walked along a small trail Lez had made with her friends. They would do things like this on their drunk days. I think they were inspired by the go-kart trail I'd made. But mine was way cooler and much longer.

"You hear that?" Tori asked again.

I couldn't hear anything, and then I saw it. And Tori was gone. And a gloomy haze swallowed the woods. The green became a muddy splash of neon light in a waterfall of colors. Through the waterfall, a Christmas tree came into focus and its blue and orange and pink and red Christmas lights oozed and leaked out of the fog and the haze and smoky white emitted from strands of white bulbs hanging down floor to ceiling from some spiraling staircase. There were guests dressed in elaborate outfits walking up this spiral staircase. Men in tuxes. Women in long black dresses. I followed them up the stairs and asked them where Tori was. They wouldn't answer me and ignored my existence. Could they even hear me? And they kept moving in their slow way, step-by-step to wherever it was they were blindly heading.

"Tori!" I called. She didn't answer.

At the top of the staircase, I saw a ballroom polluted with grainy and smoky white light coming off more of those floor-to-ceiling strands of bulbs. Massive gold chandeliers hung from the ceiling, and they bled a brilliant silver crystal mist that permeated throughout the ballroom. It was filled with people dancing and the band played on a slightly elevated platform. The piano man, dressed in a white dinner jacket, had his head buried in the keys and the tune he was playing. It was dreamy and passive and melodic. And the collective drift of the dancing guests swayed this electric mist and the Christmas wreaths in the shape of snowflakes bled out into the ballroom as their rainbow-colored Christmas tree lights competed with the dry white light raining down from the chandeliers above. I moved my way through the crowd and found myself walking down a narrow hallway with mirrors on both sides of the walls. Art deco fixtures and thick black wires connecting the bulky rainbow-colored Christmas lights ran down the staircase like a ceaseless current of color into a bar with more of those fixtures and a TV playing football hanging from the ceiling and a neon blue and red bowtie-shaped Budweiser sign right beside it and a neon yellow and red and blue Miller Genuine Draft sign to the left of that, all seeping into each other's luminescence. The liquor bottles lit from below gave off that contrast only seen in some Toulouse-Lautrec painting and all the color disintegrated into this slow current of a dream. I moved past the bar to some jazz club in the back with the solitary and very singular cocktail tables and those big orblike table lamps leading me to the small stage where the band played below an icy and powdered blue neon sign that read *Sonata Jazz*. The blue light clouded them, and I had to look through it to see them playing their instruments methodically in that trance of theirs, lost in the music and that light, it seemed. I moved away from them so as to not be lost in the blinding blue light, and I walked into a table. A hand stopped me from falling backward.

"Excuse me," I said as a thank you.

"Hard to see in here, isn't it," the man said. His face eventually penetrated through the light pollution.

"Father Lawrence," I said, seeing this man was the priest at our local church.

"Oscar," he said, shaking my hand. "Sit. Sit."

I sat and Father Lawrence's face was lit like a jack-o'-lantern by the light splashing up from the orb table lamps. He had that Toulouse-Lautrec face.

"Father," I said. "What's happening? Where am I?"

"You're in the woods," he answered.

"The woods?"

"Yes, the woods."

"Where's Tori?"

"Who's Tori?"

"My girlfriend."

"Oh, your girlfriend. I haven't seen her."

"Father?" I asked.

"Yes, Oscar?"

"I worry."

"About what, Oscar?"

"The caretakers."

"The caretakers?"

"What they've done to my grandmother."

"Your grandmother is a strong woman. Her faith is strong, too."

"She goes every Sunday."

"I know."

"I wish I did."

"God isn't just at the church."

"Is he here?"

"In the woods?"

"Yes."

"He's everywhere. Your faith is everywhere. It follows you where you go."

"I worry Lez is taking away my faith."

"Faith in yourself? Or your faith?"

"My faith."

"Why would you say that?"

"Well, she has a way."

"Oscar, we are living in different times now."

"I know."

"And you have to adapt to it."

"I know."

"Do you?" he asked.

The room felt different. The bulbs of the red Christmas lights began to flicker like stars slipping silently behind drifting moon-soaked nighttime clouds and I saw the stuttering river of brake lights. All the lights then turned green, and I had the sudden sensation of falling and the priest wasn't there to catch me. I could hear my grandmother calling me. And I could hear Tori calling me. Tori was crying. I knew it was her, but it didn't sound like her. There was a maturity in her voice—a directness in it. That of an adult. A Tori I hadn't met yet. Through that thin linen film, I could hear that mature Tori voice coming from that silhouette. "He Stopped Loving Her

Today" played in the background. Another silhouette came into view on the other side of this linen wall.

"He can't hear it," it said.

"He can," she said, sobbing. "I know he can."

The linen then became patches of dark green and I found myself falling through the leaves of the trees. I kept falling and falling and falling with that soft brush of the leaves and that tunnel of green. And there was my grandmother. At the end of that tunnel. And I clawed away at the leaves to make them turn to linen and tried to scrape through this linen to enter the room of the silhouettes and the voices. After each attempt, my grandmother would get closer to me. Until she was right in front of me, and I felt her gravitational pull—that force she used to have before Lez and Rudge. And she tore my hands away from the linen.

"Get out of the woods," she screamed in an endless echo.

"Get out of the woods."

"Get out of the woods."

"Get out of the woods."

I stopped falling through the leaves and landed on the ground with Tori's face hovering over me.

"You passed out," she said, holding my head up.

"I did?" I asked, groggy and confused.

PART TWO

Victory

"PARIS. JUNE 14, 1940," my grandmother would say in her room in her bed as she began her decline. Her past was her future, and my future was her past. That's what happens when an old woman has lived long enough to die before dying and a young man has yet to live long enough to live before living. When both misfortunes meet in the middle—the life of death and the death of life—you get someone like me listening to a senile woman tell the same story about wartime Paris. The memory would play over and over, day in and day out, until eternity would begin and end . . . would begin and end . . . would begin and end. We were now simple vessels of recollection. I, the soundboard. My grandmother, the sound. And hearing that sound time and time again, I would form my own story from her mind, and I would live in it as she mumbled on, narrating this forever of hers, this forever of mine.

◆

When Tori visited the property, I was freed from my grandmother's past—that toxic collection of memories sprouting up like weeds in the open landscape of my reality. And it was open. And Tori made sure I knew that. I was in control. And I had talent. And she would be there to help me succeed and grow and become. My grandmother would've wanted that for me too. But this shell of her didn't want that. This shell wanted me to stay back with her in Paris.

Tori was set to land at 3:20 p.m. one day, and I was getting ready to pick her up from the airport. My grandmother was somewhere in the house, and I shouted from the driveway that I would be back. On the drive over to the airport, I thought about the logging that had been done on the property. My grandmother had a lot of luck with it, and I thought she was using the money to update the house and a few of the buildings around it. The barn needed a lot of work and my grandmother said for years she had wished she had the spending money to do the job right. She'd made a lot of money from logging this year, so I thought this was the year of fixing up the barn. I even thought I'd convinced her to get rid of Lez and Rudge. Turns out it was just another year Rudge and Lez would find a way to siphon off that money. What a horror this all was.

"Osky!" Tori cried as she ran to the car. She put her head through my open window to give me a kiss. She then raced around the front of the car and hopped in and buckled her seatbelt. She was very serious about her seatbelt since her aunt had died in a car crash. I was a little less careful, which was strange since I was on my way to becoming a professional driver.

We shoved off.

"Guess what," I said with a sad clown look on my face.

"What?"

"Just guess."

"Come on. I can't."

"Why not?"

"There's a million and one things to guess."

"What's the worst thing you can think of?"

"The worst?"

"Yes."

"Like ever?"

"Like ever."

"Hmmm. Give me a hint."

"Nope."

"Fine," she said. "Rudge and Lez are still here."

"Bingo."

"Noooooo."

"Bingo."

"Come on."

"Bingo."

"I know you're lying."

"I'm not."

"That doesn't even make sense."

"It doesn't."

"I thought your grandmother didn't have the money to pay them?"

"She made some money."

"You mean on the logging?"

"Exactly."

"And she's . . ."

"Yup. She's using that money to pay them."

"Oh my gosh."

"To pay them even more."

"Noooooo."

"Yes."

"How do you know that?"

"I saw them. They drove in when I was leaving to pick you up."

"I just can't even . . ."

"Yeah."

"I'm so sorry," she said, rubbing the back of my neck. "I know how much of a drain they are."

"Are you mad at your grandmother?"

"I mean, I wish she'd told me."

"I hear you."

"She could've just told me. I mean, it's not about me. We've got a lot going on. My racing schedule next year is going to be insane.

You know that. I'm just worried about her. Lez is like a drug to her. She knows Lez is bad, but she can't stay away from her. I think Lez is a form of security for her even though she does nothing to help her. It's a bad situation."

"You nailed it."

"I worry about her."

"I know you do."

"I'm worried she's not going to survive Lez."

"Oh, Osky, she will."

"No, seriously, Tori."

"I'm being serious."

"What she becomes when Lez is around."

"I've seen it. I know. But what can you do? Worrying doesn't help."

"I can burn their goddamn house down."

"Oscar!"

"What?"

"Don't let them win like that," she said. "Don't let them ever turn you into something you're not. All that talent you have, down the drain. All on talentless people. Don't let them win like that."

"I suppose I won't."

"I suppose you won't."

"You know I was kidding."

"It's not about that."

"What is it about then?"

"The fact you even said it. The fact it even went through your mind. Joking aside."

"Tori," I laughed. "A lot of things go through this mind."

"We all know you're not exactly normal."

"Normal is boring."

"It is," she said as she leaned over to kiss me.

We exited the highway and drove through some windy backroads. I liked to have a little fun with these roads and Tori would lean back, relaxed, because she trusted my driving no matter how out of control

I got. Because I was always really in control when it came to driving. It was the one thing I knew how to do well. My brain was tactical, and my driving was tactical. And the emotions from the energy of the engine would meet with this precision of thought and create the ultimate in kinetic art. Through this creativity on wheels, I felt at home in acceleration and speed was my state of bliss. And it was now Tori's too. And in this bliss, we would thereafter live such a wonderfully fast and happy life together.

My grandmother wasn't around when we got back to the house. Lez was eating at the kitchen counter, and she waved hello with food stuffed in her mouth. Tori waved back and then rolled her eyes at me. We went straight out through the back door even though we had every intention of hanging out in the kitchen. Lez had a way of being in the places you didn't want her to be.

"She's omnipresent," Tori said to me. "What do we do now? I'm a little hungry after the flight."

"We go back in."

"I would rather get a return flight."

I laughed and held her.

"She won't want to talk to us," I said. "If we sit at the table with her, she'll get up. I promise."

"You promise?"

"Yes, I promise."

We went back into the house and Tori sat at the table as I rummaged through the refrigerator.

"Hey," Lez said. "I'd get you something but I'm on my lunch break. Been working like a dog."

I could see Tori roll her eyes in her mind.

I could hear a steady beeping, setting the pace of "He Stopped Loving Her Today" by George Jones.

◆

"Jeanne is willing to pay us properly now," she said and leaned in over the table. "At least closer to what we deserve. You know, Rudge and I have been working since we were both fifteen."

"That so," Tori said with a smile.

"It is so."

"Well, good for you."

Lez leaned back and assumed victory.

"Osk," Lez went on, more relaxed, "someone was calling here. They wouldn't stop calling. Gave me a headache."

I went into Geneva's old room to check the phone. It was that number.

"Who was it?" Tori asked, concerned by my silence.

"No one," I answered.

"Oh, come on," Tori said. "You can't say no one."

"Jeeez," I muttered to myself.

"Who?" Tori asked.

"It's just . . . I thought . . ."

Tori came into the room and shut the door behind her. "What's wrong?" she asked.

"Nothing."

"Come on. Tell me."

"Nothing. Seriously."

"Who called?"

"I don't know."

"You do know."

"Why do you want to know?"

"Because I do. Please tell me."

"Uhhh . . ."

"Tell me."

"It was my mother. She doesn't stop."

"Oh, sweetie. I'm so sorry."

"Yeah."

Lez opened the door.

"Excuse me," Tori said and slammed it shut.

Lez opened the door again.

"Do you have any sense?" Tori asked her.

"Osk," she asked, looking straight through Tori, "whose number is that? Should I call the cops? There's been a lot of break-ins in the town already."

"Break-ins?" Tori asked, outraged. "Where the hell did you hear that?"

"Down the road," Lez answered. "Just the other week."

"That's just not true. Is this what you say to Osk's grandmother to make her think she needs you? Implanting the paranoia in that old woman's heart."

Lez wanted to hit Tori. I could see it in her face. But she didn't. Because that would have given me the ammo to finally get rid of her for good.

"It was my mother," I answered to diffuse this heat.

"Your mother?"

"Yes."

"And you just ignore your mother?"

"Yes."

"I don't have a mother. You're lucky to have one."

"Not this one."

"My mother died of cancer. That means I can very well have cancer when I'm older."

"I guess so."

"You guess so. You should be ashamed you're ignoring your mother."

Tori broke down crying because Lez had a way of making her

feel so unhinged. I remained neutral like I always did. I absorbed the blows through my cushioned passivity.

"What's with her?" Lez asked, staring down at Tori, who was on the floor.

"You are such a horrible human being," Tori screamed.

"I don't ignore my mother. If I had one, I would jump into her arms."

"How about a drug addict?" Tori continued to scream. "How about a drug addict with HIV? Would you jump into her arms?"

"I would," Lez answered, folding her arms together and repositioning her stance. "And that's sad she has HIV. Poor old Rudge has ADD. Has had it all his life."

Tori jumped off the ground and scared Lez. Nose to nose, she spoke into Lez's face.

"You fuck," Tori snarled and then ripped her face away.

"I don't get paid to be abused," Lez said and went back into the kitchen. "I'm telling Jeanne about this. I don't get paid enough to be talked to like this. You White people and your White problems. Disgusting pigs."

Lez was White. And I later found she even went to one of the best all-girl private schools in Manhattan. It was called the Brearley School, I think. I went to a public school in Sullivan County with a graduation rate of 40 percent.

A lot changed in the following years. Tori graduated from the social work school at Fordham University and now shared a small apartment in the city with her best friend from that school. Her name was Lydia, and she liked me, so I liked her. That's all it took for me to like someone since it was easy not to like them. Because many people didn't understand my career. The whole racing thing. Even though I had just been signed with Willi Weber's MTS Formula Three team and I was competing in the German Formula Three series, people seemed to still think I was a kid in an adult's body, unable to get a real job. Whatever, I guess. That's what I thought to myself when I was traveling all over the world. I thought about my grandmother a lot. How she was totally detached from Lez and Rudge but still paid them and let them live there. I would also think about Tori and her crazy casework stories. She traveled all over the city to do home visits.

It was a tough job, having to go to Coney Island at 5 a.m. every Thursday. I couldn't imagine getting up at that time to visit a family that dreaded seeing me because they knew their kid was impossible to control. Tori dealt with teenagers and, sometimes, the parents. She would really deal with the whole family. And she was so modest about it. She never made it about her. It was always about the job and what had to be done. My grandmother always said she was a "real soldier" when it came to her responsibilities. There was a sense of duty, and that was a very rare word these days. Very rare. The more common words were entitled and smug and vain. I was so used to those words and the people who represented them. They hardened me into the focused racer I was now. I was trained to ignore those around me and think only of my driving and how to be better at it.

"Let's go to that hunt club," Tori said to me on the front porch of the house. "Your grandmother always talks about it and we never go."

"Well, we don't hunt," I laughed.

"Do people really hunt there?"

"Yes," I laughed again.

"Whatever. Let's just check it out."

"I haven't seen Mr. Matches in forever," I said to myself. "I wonder if he's still the president of the club."

"Time to find out."

"Hopefully he's still alive."

"Osk!"

"He's a big boy, Tori."

"I'm sure he's fine. And I'm sure he's still president of the club."

We got into my car and Tori drove. I was glad she saw it as her car because I liked making her happy and I liked seeing her use the things I gave her. It gave me satisfaction. Like I was providing for her. I felt like a man.

"It's down . . . ?" she asked.

"Down the Gail Road."

"So, turn . . . ?"

"Turn right on Crumley Van Vactor Road."

"Yup. Yup. I remember."

"Do you?" I asked and laughed.

"Shut up," she said and hit me. "I do."

"I'm kidding with you. Who can remember these roads anyways?"

"Your grandmother."

"My grandmother could do this blindfolded."

"I bet she could."

"She could."

"Your hands," Tori commented.

"What about them?"

"Full of dirt."

"Grease."

"Are you always in an engine?"

"I'll soon have mechanics doing it all for me."

"How 'bout that."

"I think about it every day."

"Me too."

We pulled into the hunt club, also known as Match House. Ever since Marshall Matches became president of the club, he had managed to raise more than any of the previous presidents combined. The woods were better. The animals were healthier. And it was safer. Much safer. He believed firmly in rules and following those rules till the end. There wasn't a three-strike policy here. It was one strike and you're out. Three longtime members had already been kicked out of the club and the other members respected Marshall Matches for it. They knew he was making this a better place. And he was also pushing the club into the future. My grandmother was their first female member, and this was met with some resistance, but everyone had respect for my grandmother, and she was more of a man than most men, so they accepted it and moved on. Anyway, due to the good radical changes, a few of the board members decided to nickname the club Match House. It wasn't officially called that. But for those who knew, it was always called Match House, not the hunt club. Tori and I called it the hunt club out of habit.

Match House, architecturally, was nothing special. It was a prefab doublewide with a big American flag on top of it with a smaller flag next to that of the club's logo. The logo was green deer antlers against a white and blue background, and Tori and I looked up at this flag through the partially windowed roof as we entered the main bar space where Marshall Matches sat smoking his Marlboro red cigarettes. He was pleased to see us and quickly put the cigarette box into the breast pocket of his jean shirt and smashed his glowing-tipped cigarette into an empty glass. Smoking was not something Marshall Matches did in public.

"Hi, Mr. Matches," Tori said and gave him a hug. He remained seated because it took him too long to get up.

"The Beauty of Sullivan County I've heard so much about," he said and kissed her cheek. "Well, just from Jeanne—but nonetheless. She's the voice of Sullivan County."

I leaned down to say hello and he grabbed my arm and pulled me in to give me a great big hug.

"The speed racer," he said, laughing with that cigarette laugh.

I righted myself and smiled and put my hands in my pocket. The club would always greet me with that same smell. It was like wet wood that had suddenly been dried and because it was dried the evaporated dampness would penetrate your sinuses and you would take in the wood walls with lumber stamps still on them. I felt uncomfortable at the hunt club. Rather nervous. I had felt that way since I was a kid, and it never went away. I'm sure Marshall Matches saw me as the nervous type even though I wasn't. It was just the club that did it to me.

"Take a load off," he said, kicking the chairs out from under the table with his legs. "Coffee?"

"I'm fine," Tori said.

I said no by shaking my head.

"How 'bout a beer?" he asked.

We both said yes to that.

"Fantastic," he answered. "We got some of that fancy beer now. IPA. I'm fine with my Coors but some of the younger members love those IPAs. So, we got some. And you're gonna try it because I won't drink it. And you're young and young people like it."

"Sounds delicious," Tori said. "Thank you."

"It's from one of them fancy breweries out somewhere yonder. Strange name. And the cans are even stranger. Kooky designs to 'em. Damn good artistry, I have to say. Something like 3 Floyds or something like that. I think that's the name. Anyways. Let me get you some. Marlene! You around? Marlene. Some beers. That IPA stuff for the kids."

"3 Floyds?" Tori asked.

"Yes, I think so."

"That's so funny."

"How's that?"

"I know that brewery. Right near my parents' house. It's in Munster, Indiana. What are the odds."

"See, all the kids know about it. And you live right there. We're modernizing. You gotta modernize in this world or you might as well go away for good. Into the woods or something and never come back."

Marlene came over with two cans of the beer.

"See that," Mr. Matches said to us. "Crazy-lookin' beers."

The cans were cool looking. It was called Zombie Dust Undead Pale Ale and a creepy-looking green zombie king was on the front against a blood-red backdrop. I kept the can for a long time.

"Zombie dust," I said and took my first sip.

"You like?" Mr. Matches asked.

Tori took a sip, too.

"Yum," she said.

"That's pretty damn good," I said.

It was good.

"Everyone your age loves it," he said. "Not really my thing, but it's not about me, right? It's about you youngsters—the future of this club. For me, I'm confused by all of it. Coors is good enough. Even coffee. I'm confused about that too. Marlene's simple medium roast morning drip does it for me. Now you have that pumpkin spiced infused . . . whatever the hell it is . . . mocha latte . . . whatever. I like a simple coffee and a simple Coors. Did it for me then. Does it for me now. Well, enough about me. How's it going up at the farm?"

Tori let me answer.

"As good as it can be," I said.

"As good as it can be?" he asked. "What the hell does that mean?"

"Rudge and Lez . . ."

"Rudge and Lez," he said to himself and exhaled through the constricted whistling airholes of his nose. The wooden chair creaked like all wood chairs do when a heavy person shifts around in them, and he flapped his light brown suede jacket for some ventilation. He always wore his World War II veteran hat, and his polarized aviators sat snug against the brim. I could almost see his eyes through their transparent state but the sheets of light coming through the blinds darkened them and hid his emotions, just as he wanted.

"Rudge and Lez," he repeated and went on. "I've never met them. Heard about them. Never met them. But people like that, through my deduction, they tend to go about this world with nothin' but what they know. You're in their casino, son. And you ain't ever gonna win. Dangerous kind of people. Treacherous kind of people. And your grandma-ma can't figure it out. God, she came to me. Sat right where you are. Confused. Dazed. Mesmerized by the mystery of Rudge and Lez. And I'm gonna tell you something. And you're not going to like it. Either of you. I can see how you feel about them. It bleeds through your eyes. But that's how they exist—through your eyes. So, stop bleedin' through them. And I'm gonna tell you something. And it's that your grandma-ma needs them."

After he said this, he could see I was disengaged from the conversation. I conveyed that by looking at my feet and cupping my hands together.

"Listen," he attempted to grasp at my fleeting attention, "she needs them. What you gonna do. You have a career. Everyone around here knows about your racin'. And you have a beautiful girl by your shoulder—and everyone knows that, too. So, all you can do—all that's left for you to do—what you can do is help your grandma-ma by not helping her. And you couldn't even if you wanted. Kid, you can't fix old problems without moving on to new ones. And they're the problems she needs. Even with all that hate in them . . . she needs them because they're the only ones around to do it. I know this because I know your grandma-ma. At the house once, when we had coffee, I asked her how she felt about them. She told me she really needed them—for the sake of the property. I asked if she was lying. She told me I was an idiot if I ever thought she would tell me the truth, but she was relieved now because she didn't have to lie. Knowing your grandma-ma, you couldn't help but know she wasn't lyin' when she said something like that. And listen, I'm not sayin' they're the right people. I'm sayin' they're the only option in this crappy mess we find ourselves in. It's what your grandma-ma knows to be the state of her present reality. And it's what I know as her reality, too. God, I think about people like that. No religion in them. Sinister people. Pessimists eatin' up the world around them. Wearin' the world around them like a scarf. Drapin' it over them as a luxury item. They think the world looks good on them. Not that they look good in it. Those are the ones who walk the land now. The ones who think they're the first to do just about anything. The first to have babies. The first to have jobs. My grandson makes me feel like I've never had kids before. What he does with his kid. Those nap schedules. The proper temperature. He came out fine, right. We had no temperature—only hot or only cold . . . and he's fine. And I love him. But it's all about him and what he has to do. Nothin' bigger than that. And for that, I believe—oh I believe—he's the last of humanity . . . the end of the line. They think they're the first to do everything. No, they're missin' it 'cause they're the last. Cause they're a generation that can't look before birth and look after death. They live holistically for what's right in front of them. And, like coffee, they burn the crap out of what's right in front of them because it's all for them and no one else. I feel useless around my grandson. I feel irrelevant. Maybe I am. But he makes me feel it more than anyone else. That generation. Got no religion. Just them. No one else but them. But this is what we have now. This is the workforce. The people that work on this hunt club, too. I can't get the damn painter here. It's like I work for him. One week he can't come 'cause of the weather. The next week he can't come because he's sick. The next, who the hell knows what happens next. I haven't got there yet. But I'll tell you both when I get there. Because I sure believe there'll be an excuse then, too. Damn truth. A hard truth. But we got no one else. I can't paint for shit. Couldn't if I tried. Can't move like I did. Can't move at all, really. Just an old war veteran sittin' in a hunt club talkin' away the days. Talkin' and talkin' and talkin'. No, you gotta understand, Rudge and Lez are necessary. If they left that would be the end of it. Whether it's healthy in the first place to keep it running, I don't know. You would know more than I. I couldn't tell you that. But you already know the answer. It's written on you. So, I won't talk on it more. Like I do with just about everything else. Time-passing talk. And you're racing away with Tori by your side. The young life. I can see the religion in you both. Whether you think you have it or not. It's there, right in you. That fire. That belief. That understanding that it all goes on after you. You're a part of something bigger. That it isn't all meaningless out there. And that's why you guys won't last here. This land don't want you and you can't go on thinking it does. Because that'll make it want you like it wants Rudge and Lez and you're better than that. It's their time now and there ain't nothin' you or I or Tori or your grandma-ma can do about it. The land wants something else livin' on it now. None of us like it but it's not our choice. A new generation has been picked by this earth. Too bad you're alone in it—in that apocalyptic feeling they all bring with them. No one else like you in your generation. Not one. Not that I've seen. The shape of things. Where we're at. Who we depend on now . . . I don't see no passion, do you? You feel like it's the edge of the cliff. We're at the end. This is the last day I burn the shit out of that coffee, like I do every day. This is the last day I do that. I won't be sittin' drinking burnt coffee no more. Last of those days. Just waiting for painters to come. Every day a no-show day. Working somewhere else, I guess. No follow-through. No honor on the word. If you say you'll be here Friday, then I expect you to be here on Friday. Not the following Monday late in the day. That young plumber does that. He just shows up at five p.m. I told him no later than four. Then he shows up with all his shit and walks through the door at five like nothin' was ever said. He isn't being a smart one. He just doesn't even know. I can see that in the smile he gives me as he walks in. Like I should be honored he came to my place that day when he did. That kid is a member of this hunt club. His daddy—a great man—got him in. And I didn't have anything against him, you know. Until I had him as my plumber. Then I knew who he was. His word as shifty as a kite in the wind. But I need him. There's no one else out there. The good ones retired, and the younger good ones are doctors and lawyers because their daddies worked dawn to dawn makin' sure they'd become doctors and lawyers.

"And that's why Rudge and Lez are more meant to be here than even you and Tori are. You'll be leavin' soon, you know that. When the racing takes you other places and Tori follows you around the world. You'll be going to that next level. We all know that. Best racer we've seen. Been cheering you on all these years. Watching you zip by front of the pack. Always front of the pack. Saw you come in second once. That's it. Says something about you here. About how long you and here are gonna be a thing. Rudge and Lez don't have that racing ability in them. They have nothing in them. This is their place more than you know. This land was always goin' to them. It was waitin' to get to them. Because it has no other options, and they have nothin' to them. The moment of nothin'-ness. The void of all things. Like the end of time. Long ago. When I would go up that stream for trout. Catching the fish. Bringin' them back here for the catch of the day. That's what we did back then. And still sometimes now. But less of it. Less of everything. A moderation of behavior I've never seen before in my days. Holding back on living like I never seen. Watch out for this. Watch out for that. Less of this. Less of that. Even the fish. Those trout. Where the hell they gone? The members of this club—where the hell they gone? They haven't left but they ain't here. The community ain't here no more. More of them stay at their houses. Watch the TV. Football. They know the players' names better than they know their family's names. Football game to football game. Then not showing up to paint houses in between. Don't see how any of the money is made, but that beats me. It's that 'dog ate the homework shit' that's floodin' us.

"But I'm glad you two came to the hunt club and visited me. I'm glad for that. Out of all the people who are busy, I get the world-famous racer and the overworked social worker from the Big Apple. Lots of problems there. Means lots of work for you. We need more of you two, you know. More than ever. That religion in you. Driving you to do great things. Making yourself bigger than yourself. You both need to get the hell out of this town. Far away. Leave it for Rudge and Lez. Leave it for me waitin' for that damn painter."

"What you talkin' to these youngsters about?" the manager of the hunt club asked. She had a pot of coffee in her hand and walked like a penguin to pour Mr. Matches a cup.

"Oh Wendy, just talkin' at them," he answered as the hot coffee drained from the pot into the cup. The steam rose from the muddy water and Mr. Matches's face, including the hat with the tinted aviators, disappeared behind the mist.

"That's what you do, Marshall," she said.

"Been doin' it for years."

"Why would you change now?"

"Why would anyone change now?"

"That's what you do, Marshall—think."

"Nothin' else left to do."

"Catchin' them trout. Shootin' them deer."

"Ahhh, they can wait."

"Anything can wait to be shot."

"It wouldn't do a damn thing anyways. Too many of them. Less of the trout. But more of them deer. Overpopulation. We're overmatched."

"Then you gotta get going on them."

"After this coffee."

"Coffee?" she asked Tori.

"No, I'm fine with the beer," Tori answered. "Thank you."

"Coffee?" she asked me.

"I'm fine," I answered.

She walked away with that walk of hers. I didn't know how people like that ever moved if it looked so unnatural for them to go from one end of the room to the other. I could never imagine being that immobile.

"Oscar," a young voice said after the front door opened.

I turned to see it was Chris Burch from my school.

"Chris," I answered. "How's it?"

"The man himself," he said, shaking my hand firmly. "The town celeb."

"I guess so."

"You'd be guessing right. Hear you're going off to Europe."

"Soon enough."

"Isn't that something. Well, finally this shitty little town is producing something."

"Hey now," Mr. Matches growled.

"Sorry," Chris retreated. "You know what I mean."

Tori caught his eye, and you could tell he was taken by her.

"Hi," he said and shook her hand softly.

"Hello," she said. "I'm Tori. Osk's girlfriend."

"Holy cow," he said, slapping at his legs. "Oscar man. You da man, man."

"All right, all right," I said, annoyed and embarrassed.

"No, seriously. Nice to meet you, Tori. Pleasure."

She nodded her head and then looked at me.

"Anyway," Chris said and twisted his body toward Mr. Matches as his shoes screeched against the fake tiled floors. "Marshall, I just picked me up one of those Yamahas and something reaaalll special for you specifically. What ya know, got it right here, in fact."

He put a can of beer on the table and Mr. Matches looked at it.

"Before you ask what it is, let me tell ya. That's a very special beer right there. Something I could only get on eBay. Think on that."

"Beers on eBay?" Mr. Matches asked. "Such a thing."

"That right there cost me a good ole ninety bucks."

"Why in the—"

"Before you go off, try it."

"Not gonna have it now."

"When you're ready, you'll know why I spent ninety bucks on it."

"I don't care how—"

"Trust me."

The tall can had an ornate label. The letters K and J were made from an elaborate display of hops and some sort of green vines and a hand inside a circle pointing to one of the hops. It was a double IPA. "KING JJJULIUSSS" it was called. I don't know why there were three Js and three Ss.

"I don't trust you," Mr. Matches responded. "A man who spends—"

"Oh, come on. Trust me. I'll get more for you when I find my way over to the brewery. It's in Charlton, Massachusetts. But I'll make my way. You can only buy direct from the brewery. But that didn't stop me. I had to get you one. So, that's why I resorted to eBay. Best beer in the world. For you. Cost me. But you're worth it. You cost me because you're worth it to me. See what I mean? And now that I have this world's best beer for you and I got me those Yamahas, I'm a happy, happy man. Happy as can be."

"Yamahas?" Mr. Matches asked, both displeased and disgusted.

"Yeah. A nice one. A blue one. A sport ATV. A Yamaha YFZ450R to be exact."

"How much is that thing?"

"Not in the mind right now to talk money."

"How much?"

"I financed it. I know what I'm doing."

"Do you?"

"I came here to get some huntin' done."

"Then go huntin'."

"I plan to."

"Planning is always good. For a man your age, it's very good."

"I used to have one of them Yamaha Banshee beasts. Think it was 350cc or something like that. Two-stroke. A violent thing. Nearly crushed my head—twice. Sold it. Then got another two-stroke bitch of a thing. Think that was called the Blaster or something. Quick little thing. Nearly crushed my head on that I'd say a good four or five times. Oh, then I got me one of them Polaris Predators. Holy cow. Five hundred cc of fun. Sold that. Now I got me the YFZ."

"That's all very nice," Mr. Matches answered.

"It is. It is."

Silence settled in and Chris awkwardly went to the lockers to change. He came out in full camouflage gear and face paint, which wasn't entirely necessary for deer hunting. But he liked the look so I would give him that. But Mr. Matches wouldn't. Anything that was done too much always annoyed him and he didn't look pleased when he saw Chris come out like that.

"Well..." Chris said, terrified by Mr. Matches' glare. "I'll be seein' ya on the other side."

I didn't know what he meant by that, but Tori and I still said goodbye. When the door shut and Chris was out of Mr. Matches' sight, our conversation began again. Mr. Matches wanted to talk to us a little more to get the bad taste out of his mouth.

"Tori," he said. "Tell me what's going on—I want to know all about the job."

"I'm—" Tori attempted before Mr. Matches interrupted her.

"I'm sorry," he said. "I just can't help myself. That boy."

"What about him?" Tori asked, not offended. It was hard for Tori to get offended.

"Talkin' about those ATVs. He has no money. He reminds me of his father. Has no father now. And I'm sure this boy will do the same to his boy."

"He has a kid?" I asked.

"Oh yes. You didn't know...?"

"No."

"A boy. Tommy, I think. Poor kid. No mother. Damn shame. A damn mess is what it is. Buys ATVs and he can't even pay for working toilets. He's invited me to his mess of a place up the road. A trailer. No heat. No air conditioning. Fans everywhere. And the smell of rotting food. The bears are around that place like deer. He complains about them but does nothing to stop what's attracting them. He only knows how to complain. He never learns. You know how much that gear he has costs? Do you?"

Tori and I looked at each other and shrugged our shoulders.

"Guess," Mr. Matches demanded.

"A hundred," I answered.

"Six hundred," he said. "I don't even have gear like that, and I've been doing this for however long I've been doing this. A long time.

He doesn't have the money for gear like that. Hell, I don't. And he still does it and goes further into debt. What in the name is the kid gonna do? How's he gonna eat? Sleep? How? A mess is what it is. And the damn assjack has big ole plasmas all over the walls. Sixty-five-inch screens. That LED stuff. Real deal. And he complains he doesn't have money for proper cool air and proper heat—and working toilets. The toilets don't flush. I've been there. A damn mess is what it is. Hell for that poor child of his. Passing on the torch of broken families. That boy had no family so why should he offer a family to his son. That's his thinking. Going out huntin' in six-hundred-dollar gear when he can't fix a goddamn toilet and asks me for money to get proper clothes for his son. Then he has the balls to walk in here with shit like that. And the dramatics he has. When he comes in here sometimes crying to me. How I'm like his daddy now. How he would be nothin' without me. Those tears in his eyes—real professional. His hands flailin' about. His eyes rollin' around in his eyes. The dramatics. That's dramatics, you know. They're all watchin' dramatics now. Going to shows. He pays for that. To go to the city. And he pays for that and has someone watch his kid for him for free—because they're doing a service to humanity by watching a poor man's kid. As he goes off to watch one of them shows. You wouldn't take him as a dramatics person. Then he uses those dramatics on me and everyone else he wants to trick. He even tricks the government—the United States of America. Gets those checks coming in like gifts from Santa. They rain in. And he doesn't care. He's not ashamed of it. Fact, he's proud of them checks. It gives him security. Like the government is the daddy he never had. 'Here, son,' the government says, 'Here's some spending money. Go wild.' Well, the government ain't our daddy. The government should be our protector of freedom and nothin' more. God's honest truth.

"You know that boy has a fulltime babysitter workin' for free—every day? He got her so tangled up in his dramatics she doesn't know what hit her. I spoke to her one day. Sayin' she should get somethin' for her time. In response, I got this blank look. Like how could I say somethin' like that to her? Because she gets a rush out of her community service. Helpin' a young man who's down on his luck. That boy has turned himself into charity. Helpin' him live a fun life is the same as feeding a starving child somewhere. She told me she was glad she could make time for him to see a show—or a movie or whatever it is. That blank look she gave. Scarier than that war look. God's honest truth. And that boy comes back to me when he doesn't have anyone else to milk the sympathy from. I swear the spotlight goes on him. They highlight his dramatics. He begs. He cries. The sweat on his face. The heavy-breathing chest. And he gives his monologue with his face contorted, moving in the strangest ways. Like opera. You know, we're a good Christian country. We forgive. We like to help without reciprocation. To even love the bad. And we surely love the bad. But I can't help myself. When I see that imaginary spotlight over that boy when he begs for my help. I'll always give him what he needs because that's how it is. I say I won't, but I do. I always do. Because that's the Christian in me. I was taught that way. As an American. The way that boy comes in here and begs. He turns the whole world around him off. It's all about him. There could be ten people in here and he'll still beg in that embarrassing way of his. And he won't care about anyone else around him. They don't exist. It's just him and me and what he needs at that moment—the rest, they can go to hell. Then the next day, I'll be out of his spotlight, and I can go to hell. Like today. Like what you just saw. As a good Christian, you'll always find yourself being taken advantage of. We're targets. Easy ones."

He placed his hat on the table.

"I fought for this country," he went on. "In that Second World War. On those beaches. I fought. And the men around me fought. I have war in my blood. None of these soul-suckers around me have a drop of war blood in them. And they're worse for it. Their blood is like swamp water. It's been sitting in their bodies too long. It hasn't bled for anything. Only for self-interest and self-preservation. They've never fought for anything besides themselves. And their blood is stagnant and corroded. God's honest truth."

The door swung open and hit the wall. Two men came in. It was Fed English and JJ Duke.

"Fuckin' mutt," JJ said and punched my arm. "Tori who's always got a story."

"Who's the fuckin' mutt?" Fed said, kissing Tori on the cheek. He shook my hand and gave me a serious man-to-man look. "JJ gets all jacked after deer huntin'. He likes to rhyme like the mutt he is."

Fed and JJ dominated the roofing business in Jersey. Any house over a million bucks, they did. And they were proud of it. But you didn't let it bother you because they were actually very good. Real talents. The stuff they could do. Mind-blowing. They had business in New York, too, but they had built their rep in Jersey.

"How's Jeanne?" Fed asked me.

"Good, I guess."

"I guess? I guess? What does that mean?"

"She's good."

"Ya see a ghost? Why you acting so spooked? Come on, I can't scare you that much."

I laughed and he ruffled my air. I did like them. They were always good to me.

"Ah, leave him alone," JJ said. "Marshall, you got any in today?"

"Haven't gone out yet."

"Ah, man. You gotta go out there."

"The old man likes sitting—reflecting," Fed said and pulled up a chair.

Mr. Matches asked if they wanted a beer, and both declined.

"How's the business?" Mr. Matches asked them.

Fed answered first.

"The business?" he answered. "Can't complain. Too bad we ain't around here no more—for the most part. This land has been had. We go off to what we call 'the hyper-rich.' Those big seven-figure

McMansions. That's all that's left these days. No nice normal folk here now. All them left and went elsewheres. Now you got here these other type of new modern people who complain about the gap between the rich and poor—and they've created that gap by just being here. Everyone wantin' to get away from them, so they go to where the work really is. You ain't part of their tribe. You ain't part of anything to them. You gotta get. So, we get to the rich. What's the word for this . . . irony, right? How 'bout that—irony. We tried. We just can't work with them no more. No comradery. No nothing. Makes the job soulless, you know. This land has been had—real had. With them. This guy—this fuckin' chum the other day. Real chum. JJ and I had a job near . . ."

He began to snap his fingers to trigger his recall.

"Near . . ."

He snapped some more.

"Where was it . . . where was it . . ."

"In Alpine," JJ answered.

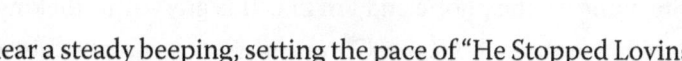

I could hear a steady beeping, setting the pace of "He Stopped Loving Her Today" by George Jones.

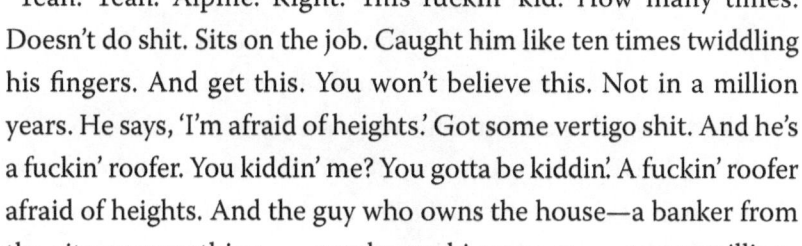

"Yeah. Yeah. Alpine. Right. This fuckin' kid. How many times. Doesn't do shit. Sits on the job. Caught him like ten times twiddling his fingers. And get this. You won't believe this. Not in a million years. He says, 'I'm afraid of heights.' Got some vertigo shit. And he's a fuckin' roofer. You kiddin' me? You gotta be kiddin'. A fuckin' roofer afraid of heights. And the guy who owns the house—a banker from the city or something . . . you know, big money . . . seven-million-dollar house we're working on—and he wants it done when we say it'll be done. And I got this finger-twiddling vertigo kid sayin' he can't climb a ladder because it makes him feel dizzy or some shit like that. Can't make this stuff up. So, finally, I was like 'Get the fuck outta here.' He looked at me like I was confused. Like I didn't mean to say that. So, I told him again: 'Get the fuck outta here.' Sittin' on the fuckin' job. Doin' nothin'. We gotta anotha one of these kids up in ahhh . . . we gotta job in Buffalo. Up near there. Fuckin' guy, man. What are these guys doin'? Sleeping on the job. Bitching. Breakfast break. Lunch break. Dinner break. Self-help break. Time-to-ponder break. The whole mental health thing. Time for me. Some shit like that every second. The job goes in between the fuckin' me-me-me breaks. It's busting my balls. JJ and I have fired four guys in one week because of this. It's ridiculous. Real shame. We don't like doing that. But these fuckin' kids, you know. And one of the mothers actually called me after I fired one of them. The kid was thirty years old. I kid you not. Thirty years old and he told his mother about it and she called me sayin' I was abusive or something and she was going to tell all the people around her not to use me for their roofs. I told her I was booked solid till the end of time, and she'd be doing me a favor. She hung up the phone and I'm like 'this guy'—this fucking kid who told his mother about me. Come on. You can't make this stuff up."

He pointed at me.

"You're not one of those fuckin' kids," Fed said. "The next Ayrton Senna we got here. What you gonna do with all those trophies when you rake them in?"

"I'll take them," Tori laughed.

"Ahhh, you better watch this one. Watch the money. The women love the money. Especially when you really have it."

"Better watch out," Tori said and kissed me.

"This fuckin' guy, you know," JJ said, jabbing his thumb in my direction. "Luckiest motha fucka I've ever seen. You know you're the fuckin' luckiest motha fucka I've ever seen? Do ya? Do ya?"

I bent Tori backward and gave her one of those dramatic kisses.

"This fuckin' guy," Fed laughed.

"Guess that's what happens when you're on your way to F1," JJ said. "Lots of green there."

"You guys aren't doing too bad yourselves," I commented.

"Always doin' good, my friend," Fed said as he winked at Mr. Matches.

Mr. Matches saw Fed and JJ as one of his own. They fixed everything for him, and Mr. Matches was a little weird about certain things with them because they refused to take money from him. We were all family.

"Oscar will be gettin' out of here soon," Mr. Matches said, admiring me like a father would. "Goin' all over Europe."

"Formula Three, right?" Fed asked.

"Yes," Mr. Matches answered for me.

"Keep it safe," JJ said.

"You'll keep it safe, right, Tori?" Fed asked.

"Under my watch," Tori said, "nothing will happen to Osk."

"Atta girl," Mr. Matches said and put his hat back on.

"You two," Fed said. "Gettin' the hell outta here. Why wouldn't ya? Jeanne is ready to dump that place anyway. It's a damn chain around your neck. Get outta here and move on. Don't let anything here slow you down, Osk. You plow through life and win races. Ya hear?"

I nodded and Tori looked at me. "Yes," I added.

"And miles to go before I sleep," Mr. Matches said.

"Come back at the end," JJ said. "Come back when you're a grandpa. Get out now like you're doin'. Fed and I got out to Europe and made somethin' outta it. Not like Europe, that Jersey. But it did a lot for us to get out."

"I think Osk is worried about his grandmother," Tori said for me.

"Jeanne?" Fed asked with confidence in his tone. "That's one tough woman. Leave it to her. Trust me."

"Jeanne taught us everything we know," JJ said. "Like Fed said, leave it to her."

Fed and JJ went to the locker room and Mr. Matches had his eyes on me. He always did that before he was going to say something to you.

"Those boys are right," he said to me. "Now, enough about Oscar. Tori, my dear. I was askin' you before about your job. Then we all got cut off with other stuff. How's the job, darlin'? You're not givin' it up for Oscar's crazy superstar life, are you? Never lose the thing that makes you, you."

"They're very flexible," she said. "I can take off when I need to."

"How work has changed," Mr. Matches marveled. "But social work is the most honest of all professions. A thankless job. You deserve to take breaks. Breaks from the craziness. People with all their problems. Everyone is twisted up but you're dealin' with the most tangled of all of them. I'm sure you have some crazy stories. Tell me a crazy story. You're not a social worker without at least one crazy story."

"Okay. Hmmm. Let me think." Then she snapped her fingers and said excitedly, "I got it. A few weeks back, Ms. Farrow came into our Brooklyn office for a session to meet with my therapist assistant, Angelo. But she insisted I be present for this session as well. Ms. Farrow expressed her need for support and case management in a long list of areas, such as her rat-infested apartment, which she was currently squatting in because she believed she 'owned' the entire building. Other areas that needed a lot of attention were her medical health issues. She insisted phone calls be made to the insurance company as they 'were not returning her calls.' I agreed to call the insurance company to get her medical insurance straightened out and, while this was going on, Angelo was asking her other follow-up questions regarding her insurance. Ms. Farrow then decided to tell Angelo about all her health problems. This is what she said to him, I promise you: 'I went to the bathroom and there was blood all over the toilet, back of the wall.' Angelo looked confused and asked, 'Oh, like you had your period?' Ms. Farrow replied to this, 'Oh no, sweetheart, the other hole.' I overheard this conversation and looked over at Angelo, whose face was absolutely horrified and amused."

Mr. Matches hadn't formed a reaction yet. I had heard this story before, so I had the same face—smiling in disbelief.

"Holy cow," Mr. Matches said, shaking his head. "And where does this Ms. Farrow live?"

"Coney Island," Tori answered.

"How long's that commute for you?"

"An hour and a half, sometimes two."

"Holy cow. When do you go to her place?"

"Have to get there by five thirty."

"Five thirty?"

"Yes."

"When do you end?"

"Usually around seven."

"Then you leave?"

"I get back home between eight thirty and nine o'clock."

"It isn't safe over in Coney Island. Not at night, at least."

"I get the catcalls every so often."

"Catcalls?"

"Yeah. Catcalling. When men whistle and shout nasty things at me as I walk by to get to the train."

"How 'bout that . . ."

"I had one follow me."

"What you do about that?"

"I always keep looking forward and, if you happen to see a cop car, run to it."

"This world. And how does your boyfriend feel about this?"

Tori looked at me and grabbed my chin. My lips squashed together like a fish.

"He knows I can handle it," she answered for me, still holding my chin.

Fed English and JJ Duke came out of the locker room and were ready to hunt. The draft they created as they rustled around in their gear showed how ready they were. You could feel off them they'd do well today. They were great hunters. Respectful, too. "In and out and never showing off," as Mr. Matches would say.

"Hey," Fed said to me, "how's that rascal doin'?"

"The dog?" I asked.

"Yeah, the dog. Ernie, right?"

"He's good. Half wild. But good."

"Spends more of his time outside being a dog. Jeanne never has him in the house."

"An outlaw," I added.

"That dog is an outlaw. Lives by his own rules out there. But a sweet dog, you know."

"He is."

"Does he come back at night?"

"Sometimes."

"What a dog."

"Got his own thing going on."

"All right," JJ said, waiting by the door. "We gotta get."

"All right. All right," Fed said and patted my shoulder. "Send us some good luck, ya hear."

"You won't need it," Mr. Matches said.

"God willing," Fed said before he shut the door behind him. The way you shut a door behind you says a lot about your character. With Fed and JJ, you never had to wince before it would crash back against the frame, and you never had to get up to fully shut it. You didn't have to worry about anything with them.

"My type of boys," Mr. Matches said, looking at the closed door.

"I know they've always been great to Osk," Tori said.

"They've been good to everyone," Mr. Matches added. "Anyway, you youngsters got anything planned today?"

"Osk is in his Halloween mood."

"How's that?" Mr. Matches asked.

"He wants to watch spooky movies," she answered.

"She's talking about like Freddy and Jason stuff," I clarified.

"Who's Freddy and Jason?"

"The movies," I answered. "*A Nightmare on Elm Street*. You know, Freddy with those razor claws. Freddy Krueger."

"Oh, yes," Mr. Matches laughed. "That's some scary stuff. You get a kick from that?"

"We both do," Tori answered. "That and all the *Friday the 13th* movies."

"*Friday the 13th*—that's the one with the hockey mask?"

"Exactly. Osky loves it. He's more of a Jason fan. And I'm more of a Freddy fan."

"What's the difference?"

"Well, Freddy comes alive in your dreams."

"Sounds horrifying."

"And Jason is kinda this undead villain. He drowned in a lake. That sort of thing."

"I'm more of a *Halloween* guy," Mr. Matches said.

"Osky and I love that, too."

"Jason sounds to me a lot like Michael Myers."

"Yeah," Tori said. "Now that I think of it, they are very similar. They both can't die. But I think Michael Myers is a little more metaphorical."

"How do you mean?" Mr. Matches asked.

"Michael Myers is like the personification of fate."

"Fancy."

"Like a force."

"I'm hearin' ya."

"Jason is just kinda undead—like an undead creature."

"You guys better be gettin' watchin' then."

This was Mr. Matches way of saying he wanted to be left alone. He would always get tired of conversation at a certain point, and I respected him for that. Sometimes people went on too long.

But right before I left, and Tori had already exited, he grabbed my arm and said, "I know how you're feelin' 'bout all of it. I know. I been there. To watch the thing you love become a memory while you still have it—it's the fastest way to ruin a life worth living. You become that ghost attached to the thing you're trying to save. You sink with it until you're so lost in yourself that you finally see the only way you could've saved it was to let it go. So, let the damn thing go. Let it go, Oscar. You've got a life to live. And it's not here. Don't bring Tori into your past, because there's no way you'll both get out. Whether you realize it or not, you're not in the majority anymore. You're the minority. And you gotta get out because you've already lost. This ain't your land no more. *They* have it. The house always wins and it's their house. And you're playing their game. They own it. Not you. You need to understand. You're now in their world—they're not in yours. There's no way you can win."

I walked out and left the door open.

Tori and I went to most of the countries in Europe. The property was a faraway dream and I made sure to call my grandmother once a week to see how things were. I was making a lot of money now and made a name for myself in the racing world. I was really heading to Formula One. It wasn't just something Tori's father would say anymore. It was real. I made my Formula One debut with the Irish Jordan-Ford team. But my grandmother was always in the back of my mind. The doctors couldn't figure out what she had. They ruled out Alzheimer's. All I knew was she was drifting, and the conversations I had with her got simpler and simpler. I flew in one week with Tori in between races. I had the money to do that now and tried to do it as often as I could.

"The lawns," Tori noted as we squeezed behind Lez's car parked at the tip of the driveway. She knew we were coming in that day.

"Where is she?" I asked. "She's usually at the porch when we pull in."

My grandmother had bounced back a little since I had become an emerging household name. She felt pride in that, and she would wait outside on the porch for us. She had the energy to do that even when she would look out onto the weed-infested, uncut lawn.

"Lez," Tori called. "Lez!"

No answer, per usual. We didn't call Rudge because he didn't exist. No one ever saw him.

We walked into the kitchen and my grandmother was sitting at the table, drooling.

"Jesus," Tori screamed. "Jeanne. Jeanne. Are you all right?"

"Lez!" I screamed.

"I'm just cleaning Torrance," she called from the garage. "Give me a second. Was in the garage getting the wax. He was so dirty, my poor Torrance."

"Lez," I screamed back. "Get the fuck up here."

That was the first time I said that to her. And there was silence after I said it. She took her time getting to the house.

"Did she have a stroke?" Tori asked me. "Did she?"

"I don't know," I answered. "Grandma. Can you hear us? Grandma?"

She was breathing but unresponsive. Her eyes were wide open.

Lez finally entered and stopped dead in her tracks when she saw my grandmother. I could tell she was trying to formulate excuses.

"I don't care, Lez," I yelled, anticipating her defense game. "Help me get her into the car."

"Not my car," Lez said, startled and selfish, in her high-pitched voice.

"No, Lez," I answered, simply tired of her, "my car."

"Shouldn't we call for an ambulance?" Tori asked.

"It'll take them twenty minutes to get here," I answered. "I can get her to the hospital in fifteen."

"They're always more responsive at hospitals when an ambulance pulls in—"

"When we bring her in like this, they'll be responsive. Trust me."

"Okay, Oscar."

"Not my just-cleaned Torrance, though," Lez added.

She really was exhausting. Such a suck of space. And she happened to be wearing one of her new annoying shirts she had gotten from this older man she was hanging out with. I knew about him because my grandmother would tell me about him on our phone calls. His name was Groak Trimms, and he was a former Louisiana state trooper. My grandmother built up her obsessive hatred of him after she found out he'd been a member of the Ku Klux Klan in Louisiana. Her friend told her he'd written a few essays on his theories of Racial Reconstruction, which my grandmother called "Racist Reconstruction" in her growing hysteria of pure anger brought on by the strengthening dementia. Everything Lez did was killing her, and soon, this hysteria would unhinge itself into a self-propelled complexity of madness brought on by the simple squeak of Groak's brakes when he parked by the barn. She confessed to me she'd bury her head into her pillow when he pulled up to the house, nearly suffocating herself each time. To even hear the brakes made her sick and violent because she knew they were owned by a man like that. I really wished she had the courage to tell Lez he wasn't allowed on the property. And it made no sense Lez was friends with a confirmed KKK member. She was such a little "freedom fighter" and there was always guilt by association. But that was just it. Nothing made sense with this new breed of people. It was a continuous layering of nonsensical realizations forming a totally original type of satirical hypocrisy. Groak would show up every day, the racist he was, so unfriendly, waiting creepily on the back of his truck for his young hot crush to arrive. They'd go on long walks together and they'd walk the road and stop at an old woman's house right at the edge of the property. My grandmother disliked this woman because she sold off some of her land to a corrupt Hasidic Jew my grandmother had taken to court a few times. His name was Asher Blau and the land he bought was trashed and polluted and he supposedly would dump his garbage into the streams that ran into our property. This woman also knitted for his family, and they paid her well, so she did a lot of "behind-the-scenes favors" for him. No one in the town trusted her and she became very close with Lez and Groak and all three of them became very close with a lot of the Hasidic communities sprouting up in the area. (The ex-KKK member was friends with Hasidic Jews and the freedom fighter was friends with the ex-KKK member and all of them were friends with each other . . . go figure.) Was anything real anymore?

"Lez!" a man's voice said as we put my grandmother in the back seat. "Lez! Lez! Lez!"

It was coming from a man sitting on the back of his truck parked by the barn. His legs were swinging off the back of the truck and he was doing nothing to help us.

"We're taking my grandmother to the hospital," I yelled over to him.

He ignored me and called Lez one more time. And that's when I lost it. I walked over to the barn and stood in front of him, his swinging feet inches from hitting my legs. I could see through his small rear window that imposing reflective blue handicap placard dangling from the windshield mirror. My eyes then shifted back to him. Those eyelids covered in skin tags. I wondered if they impaired his vision. That plus the lack of teeth made him a hard person to be up and personal with. But that chip on his shoulder. That visceral hatred he had for the person he assumed I was—the person Lez had created in his simple mind. She brought this false existence step-by-step into his bendable reality. After each walk, he wanted more and more to hurt me, even though I was rarely there. Because there was always a spot in Groak's heart ready to be filled with anger. This is what those walks were for—building the hatred, which I saw now in its most distilled form. His eyes were feral and his reserved aggression toward me was animalistic and totally unhinged. Like a watchdog unable to fully get at me because of a rusted chain. Law and order, his chain. And it was the only thing stopping him from clawing and biting me to death. Otherwise, I was prey to him, and I was put on this planet to die by his hand. I'm sure he knew nothing about what I'd been through. How my father died for his country. How my mother became a victim of its unresolved drug crisis. I'm sure that part slipped Lez's mind. I'm sure he knew none of that. And I'm also sure he had no idea Lez was really from a lot of money and she had gone to a private school in Manhattan. I'm sure divulging that information slipped her mind.

But it was fine that it had. Because Groak was attracted to her and he waited for the day to come when those walks would turn into dates and when those dates would turn into something else. He was a linear old man with a crush. That trumped her lies even if he knew she was lying, which he didn't. To him she was hot. And I was the oppressor who made the object of his affection stressed and sad. I had brought this life to them both. Somehow, I was the reason he couldn't have her. And the fact I was successful at something. Moving on with my life. That made me the enemy in his eyes. Because nothing had ever worked out for him. Because of people. And I was those people. It didn't matter how hard I worked for my success. The fact was, I was successful at what I did. The only way I could've been acceptable to Groak was to fail and fall through the cracks through laziness and unwillingness to grind. I didn't have that cowardice disguised as underprivilege. Lez had a pass in this black-and-white land of the oppressed and the oppressor. The simple mind of a man manipulated by the complex mind of a woman is the closest thing you can get to Frankenstein's monster. And here he was, the monster. Right in front of me. Wanting to kill.

"I don't think we've met," I said, pushing these thoughts aside.

"Come on, Osk," Tori called from the car.

Lez had gone back into the house.

"I guess the name is 'Osk,'" he said with a clownish toothless smile. A toothpick poked out from between his crusted lips.

"You guess?" I asked. "You know very well it is."

"How would someone up in the castle like you know that about someone down here in the pits like me?"

"I bet you talk about us a whole lot on those walks."

"Yeah . . . yeah, Sherlock. You got me. We do. You're the racer. The big-money man who keeps it all for himself."

"So that's how you see me?"

"I know the rich folk when I see them. They leave us stranded and take up sports no one watches—like little hobbies. I don't even see it as a sport, but I'll give you that bone so you don't seem as pathetic as you really are. Poor soul, you are. Violently rich with money you don't know what to do with. And don't you racers basically buy your way in? You buy up a team to build you up and they make you win races. It's all a rich scam."

"'Violently rich'? Hmmm. Vivid."

"I smell it. Like a fungus."

"Well, wow . . . I'm glad I metaphorically smell like it because you—"

"You wanna say somethin'? Say it, pussy doll."

"Get the fuck off my property!"

He stretched his legs out so his swinging feet hit me. He kept kicking at me. Harder and harder with that toothless smile growing and growing and growing.

"Ya know whaaaaaat," he said. "Why don't you get off *my* fuckin' property, bitch."

I punched him straight in the jaw and he fell off the truck. I turned around and walked back to the car.

"What the hell is wrong with you?" Tori said, smacking my arm. "That man isn't getting up. Why would you do that? Risking everything. Our future."

"Oh, stop, Tori. That redneck? To hell with him."

"You're not like that, Oscar. Don't be like them. Don't let them change you into what they want. They want you to act like that. Don't you see?"

"Oh, stop."

"Don't tell me to stop. You punched an old man and he's still on the ground."

I looked at my grandmother slouched over like a doll and backed the car out of the driveway. Before I shifted out of reverse into drive, I saw Lez run out of the house toward the motionless Groak. She had a shirt on that read, *Every day I make history* on the front and *by being me* on the back.

"I'm disappointed in you," Tori said, crying.

"I'm getting rid of Lez," I said, my mind miles down the road. "My grandmother needs real help up here. I'm tired of this. When we get back, I'm giving Lez and Rudge the week to get their things and get out."

"Who's going to be there for Jeanne?"

"I'll find someone. It's not like Lez and Rudge help at all anyway."

"But they're there."

"And . . ."

"That's all there is to it."

"We're not paying people anymore to be neighbors. Bad neighbors in their case."

"We can't be around."

"I can try."

"Oscar, you can't. We need to fly back. Your schedule is crazy. Come on. Be reasonable. We need to keep Lez and Rudge for now. There's no other option."

"I'll think of something. There's gotta be someone up here."

"There's no one. You heard what Marshall said."

"Marshall Matches?"

"Yes."

"He's so down on everything. Don't listen to a word he says. He just talks. I grew up with him just talking. All chatter. No action."

"Don't say that. He really respects you, Oscar."

"I know he does."

"So, why would you say that?"

"I don't know."

"You always say 'I don't know.'"

"Well, I don't know."

"We need them. I know you hate them. I do, too."

"I just can't believe there's no one up here," I said, slamming my hands against the steering wheel. "How? How? How?"

"It's hard to find people who want to work."

"You sound like all of them when you say that."

"Maybe I am 'all of them.'"

"I'm sorry, Tori."

"You don't have to say you're sorry."

"I really am, though."

"I know you are. But you can't go on punching people. He wasn't moving, Oscar. He fell off that truck."

"He didn't fall off a building."

"He's an old man."

"Yeah. Well, Lez has aged me for sure. She's nearly killed my grandmother. I wonder how long she was in there like that. While that bitch was waxing that fucking car."

"Oscar!" Tori gasped. "You're better than this. Please."

"If something happens to her . . ."

"What are you going to do?"

"What am I going to do?"

"Yes."

"A bad thing."

"Oscar, there's so much for you to lose. Life is offering you so much. And you can't ruin it."

"I can't ruin it for you?"

"What?"

"You heard me."

"That's an awful thing to say," she cried. "You think I'm like that?"

I didn't respond.

"Do you think I'm like that?" she asked again.
"No, I don't."
"What a terrible thing to say."
"Tori..."
"To see you like this... it scares me."
"Tori..."
"You're becoming something I don't like."
"I..."
"If you really feel like—"
"I don't," I belted, interrupting her.

I was going almost seventy miles per hour in a thirty-mile-an-hour zone and Tori thought nothing of it. I loved that about her. How she trusted me when I was in my element. And I could never lose her. She made me, as corny as that sounds.

"I know you don't," she said, calm. She looked over at my grandmother. "How much longer?" she asked.

"Ten minutes."
"It'll be fine. It'll be fine."
"I should've been an ambulance driver."
She smiled. Then she laughed to herself.
"What's so funny?" I asked.
"Nothing."
"What?"
"I'm just thinking about a time Jeanne called me."
"She calls you?"
"Yes, of course. She can't get to you half the time."
"I need to be focused."

"Yes, I know. You need to be focused for your races. I get that. I'm not belittling you. I totally get it. And so does your grandmother. That's why she calls me."

"What do you talk about?"
Tori laughed to herself again.
"What, Tori?"

"She really doesn't like that Groak guy."

"Yeah, I know. That's why—"

"You shouldn't have done that. Anyway . . . she thinks Lez and Rudge have an open relationship. Groak is kinda like the second husband. And Rudge is fine with it."

"It wouldn't matter if he was fine with it or not. Not with Lez."

"So right. I don't think that guy has a brain."

"You think Groak does?"

"He's a writer."

She waited for me to laugh, and I didn't.

"Bad joke," she said. "I'm sorry. Anyway . . . I'm just realizing this now . . . but Jeanne told me that Groak has bladder cancer. I think they removed it or something. He's got like a bladder bag."

"A Camelbak of piss!" I announced.

"Stop," she laughed. "You're horrible. It's serious . . . what he has. Cancer isn't funny."

"You're laughing . . ."

"That was kind of funny. But seriously, I'm just realizing now . . . I think Lez became friends with him after hearing your mother has HIV."

"I don't see the connection here."

"Think about it. She was so angry when she found out your mother had HIV."

"Tori, she doesn't care about my mother. She wouldn't be angry."

"No, you're not getting it. She was angry because she didn't have something worse to deal with. You know that just as well as I do. Don't pretend to be above this 'he said, she said' drama."

"I'm not," I said, even though I was trying to be.

"I bet she hitched up with Groak to compete with you—who can have the saddest relationship."

"I'm glad you think my relationship with my mother is sad."

"You know what I mean. Jeanne told me she's been telling everyone in town about her poor old friend who's dying from cancer.

And how she's taking care of him because he has no one to take care of. She talks about his poor old wife dying a few years back, leaving him all alone. I guess no one talks about how he used to beat her and have the cops showing up every other day when she fought him off enough to get to the phone."

"Wow, you guys have really talked about this."

"Jeanne tells me everything. I find it so fascinating. How fucked up people are. Everyone is just so fucked up. Oh, my gosh . . ." She put her hands over her mouth. "The names . . ." she giggled.

"The names for what?"

"For Groak. Lez has nicknames for him."

"I can only imagine."

"You couldn't even imagine these."

"What?"

"Some days she calls him Moose. Other days she calls him Cow."

"Moose?"

"You're stuck on Moose? So, Cow is perfectly normal?"

"I'm taking one at a time."

"And your grandmother has no idea why. Lez would be in the kitchen with her talking, not doing work as usual, and then she'd look at the time—it was always four p.m.—and she'd jump up like a little girl and say it was time for her walk with Moose or Cow. How odd, right?"

"These nicknames of hers. I'm sure as a kid she had a nickname for everything. She was probably the worst child ever. Wouldn't want to be in a class with her."

"Could you imagine the bullying . . . what she did to those poor kids."

"She's a kid now so it's easy to imagine," I said. "I don't know."

"You don't know what?"

"It makes me think. We always talk about her. She's consumed so much of our life—the hatred we've built for her."

"Oh, come on, Osk. It's funny. You have to laugh at things sometimes."

"No, I know. But I wonder if she's the only thing that gives meaning to this property. I wonder if there wasn't anything good about it in the first place—before she arrived. Maybe she's a good thing. Because anything in comparison is good. Maybe, without her, the place wouldn't mean as much to me. There's no good without bad. And she's the bad. She's what glorifies the memory."

"Osk, you had a wonderful time at that house before she arrived. You did. It's just hard to remember now because Lez is so terrible. It's clouded things for you."

"Has it? Because when I think on it now, all I can remember was missing my father and watching my mother fall apart. Missing my parents and feeling lonely in that house—that's really it. I'm being honest with myself now. More honest than I've ever been."

"You're honest, Osk."

"My memories aren't real, Tori."

"Stop talking like that. What if your grandmother can hear. How would she think?"

"She can't hear."

"How do you know? We don't know what the hell is wrong with her. I've never seen anything like this—someone frozen with their eyes open."

"A stroke."

"You a doctor?"

"What else is it?"

"That's what I'm saying—I don't know."

"We're less than five minutes away from the hospital."

Tori searched her pocket for her phone and shifted her body in that wormlike way when your jeans pockets were too tight.

"Oh, God," she said. "Oh my God."

She covered her mouth.

"What? What?" I asked.

"Lez posted a picture of Groak. I think he's really hurt, Oscar."

"Did she write anything?"

"Yes."

"What did she write?"

"Oh my God."

"Tori, what did she write?"

"And the responses..."

"Tori!"

She began to cry uncontrollably and slammed her phone against the dashboard.

"What the hell, Tori," I yelled, swerving from this impulse reaction. She was always more controlled than this.

"Jesus Christ."

"I want to know what she said."

"It's just..."

"Please."

"She's calling you a murderer."

"Ahhh, jeeeez, Tori. Well, that's typical Lez exaggeration."

"She's also going off on other things. The 'slave-like' conditions of her job stuff. She's been there before but a lot of people are responding now."

"Who's responding?"

"I don't know. Her city friends, I guess."

"That crew..."

"Jesus, Oscar."

"She's always doing stuff like this on social media. Remember when she filmed that guy in that horrible bicycle accident, and she didn't even help him... just kept filming to get the viral video she always wanted. I think the cyclist died."

"This is about *you*, Oscar. Everyone hates you. Lez has hundreds of thousands of followers. You can't have this on you. Not when you're building a racing career for yourself. You can't have this stuff on you."

"Who's commenting?"

"Out of the hundreds of responses... I don't know... I see one of them is a woman in a star outfit on some weirdly lit stage—big smile. Doesn't look like she would even know how to say the things she's saying. She's saying horrible things."

"What is she saying?"

"She sent a picture of an electric chair and said you should be in it—and everyone like you."

"Show me her picture."

I looked at her profile, my eyes bouncing from the road to the screen.

"I know her," I said.

"Who is she?"

"She's been here."

"It makes no sense."

"What makes no sense?"

"She's outwardly opposed to capital punishment." I laughed to myself.

"This is not funny, Oscar."

"Oh, but it is."

"It's not."

"How can you take any of this seriously?"

"It's public. Nothing public is funny."

"I think it's funny that someone who's as vocally against capital punishment as she is is saying I should be in the electric chair. Not even lethal injection—the electric chair. About as polar opposite as you can be."

"And someone wearing a zebra outfit said you should've been aborted."

"I'm sure that person's pro-life," I laughed.

"Stop."

"Who else? Give me more. This is fun."

"Another guy in an overly tight lion outfit singing and pulling on his tail clearly hates you. Another wearing a giant wig and layers of lipstick and makeup—and I think he's wearing Elvis pants—this guy really, really hates you, Oscar. This is bad. Very bad."

"Surprise, surprise."

"This isn't fucking funny. This is blowing up."

"Groak is fine, and this is simply Lez's dramatics. She's always trying to get internet famous. You know that."

We pulled into the hospital and carried my grandmother in. A nurse walking through saw it was my grandmother and she ran to grab help and three large men put her on a stretcher and rolled her away. Tori and I sat in the waiting room across from each other because Tori couldn't be near me, not even with my grandmother in the emergency room. She was lost in her phone, and I could see from the very wet and reflective lenses of her eyes her fingers scrolling through Lez's posts. Lez had a way. She could still make a day, even one like this one, all about her.

Dr. Zeck entered the waiting room, and he was quick with us.

"She's fine," he said. "But I want her here overnight. Oscar, I think you're going to have to start thinking about assisted living for her."

"What's happening to her?" I asked.

"She has a very bad UTI and she's incredibly dehydrated. Is someone taking care of her at the house?"

"We have caretakers."

"Well, it looks like she's been grossly overlooked. Her clothes are filthy. It doesn't look like she's been changed out of them in days. She's had no water and hasn't gone to the bathroom because of it. Her brain was basically shutting down."

"I could kill her," Tori said.

"Sorry?" Dr. Zeck asked.

"The caretaker," she said.

"Jeanne needs more than a caretaker," he said, tapping his pen against his clipboard. "As I said, I think you need to take the next step."

Dr. Zeck turned around and swept out in his white outfit. He walked out of the waiting room. He was always quick that way.

When we pulled onto the road that snaked up into the property, we could see flashing red and blue lights.

"What happened?" Tori asked.

I drove at a crawling pace, summiting the top of the hill. I had a feeling. Cop cars were everywhere. An ambulance. What had I done? It hadn't hit Tori yet.

"What happened?" she asked again.

I pulled into the driveway and saw the sheriff make his way over to us. He was repositioning his hat a lot and wiping his forehead, which nine times out of ten meant something very bad had happened. I knew the sheriff well. He was a close friend of Marshall Matches and my grandmother. The hunt club was his second home, and my grandmother was his second mother. His name was Efrem Dorf. Everyone called him Dorf, including myself. He was the nicest, most unassuming sheriff the county ever had. A true gentleman.

"Dorf," I said, rolling down the window.

"Osk," he replied, tipping his hat.

"What's going on?" Tori asked.

"Tori—good to see you," he said through his half-smile, plagued to the core with this bad news. "Ahhh, Osk. It's not lookin' good. Not lookin' good at all. Groak had a bad fall. Lez said you punched him to the ground?"

"I punched him once," I answered, my eyes locked on the steering wheel. My knuckles were white against the distressed leather wrap and Dorf could see how tense I was.

"You ageist murderer," Lez barked from the front porch like this was her house. Two officers held her back and she kept screaming, "Ageist murderer. Ageist murderer. Ageist murderer!"

"All right," Dorf said, ignoring her. "Whether it was one punch or fifty, Groak still hit the ground as a result of it. He broke his neck, Osk. He's dead."

Tori fainted and Dorf called over an officer to help her out of the car. I remained frozen in my seat, my knuckles a milk white. I looked at the gear lever and saw the red light—it was shifted into park.

"Now, Osk," Dorf said, "I'm gonna need you to get out of the vehicle."

He motioned the other police officers away.

"Can you do that for me?" he asked as he placed his hand on his gun.

I wouldn't respond and my sweaty palms rubbed against the tight water-repellent steering wheel leather. Marshall Matches was right. The house had won, as it always would. And I had made Lez's dream of injustice become a reality. Something she could really talk about now without having to hide behind the truth. I was the oppressor, and she was the oppressed. I had lost.

"Osk . . . ?" he said, trying to shake me from my shock. "Can you do that for me?"

I still didn't respond. All was so lost now. Everything I'd worked for was over. With one stupid punch. And that was the first damn time I'd ever hit anyone.

"Osk . . ." he said again. "Now look—I could've had my men go straight over to the hospital. I had them wait here instead. I know this is a shitty mess, but I need you to work with me here. We can work this out together. Groak wasn't a good man—no loss for society. We all know that. But the law is the law. So, you gotta work with me. I don't want to do this the conventional way. I don't want to because I know you don't want me to. I'm really trying to work with you here, Osk. You're a friend and I wanna treat you like a friend no matter what the situation seems to be right now."

"His brake lights," one of the police officers shouted to Dorf. "They're on. He's gonna run."

"Osk, you're not gonna run. You gonna stay right here."

"He's gonna run, Sheriff."

"He's not gonna run. I know he's not gonna run."

The police officer took his gun out.

"He's gonna run," he repeated, pointing the gun at the car.

"Put the goddamn gun down," Dorf yelled. "Put it down. No one is runnin'. Right, Osk? No one is runnin'."

Then.

Suddenly.

Into reverse.

The wheels spun.

The car whipped around.

Into drive.

The wheels spun again.

Smoke in the air.

That vaporized rubber.

That smell.

How much I loved it.

Then I was off.

The needle bouncing off the redline.

No braking.

Using friction as my guardrail.

Left to right, right to left.

Sliding through tight bends.

The sound of cop cars chasing me disappearing into the trees.

They knew they could never catch me.

A hundred and twenty miles per hour in a thirty.

Impossible.

I would get the hell out of here.

Never come back.

Tori would find me.

Somehow.

Somewhere.

Then.

There it was.

I had to brake.

But I wouldn't.
The momentum would overtake the downforce.
I knew that.
But I wouldn't brake.
Never again.
Not in this lifetime.
"Shit," I said to myself.
I turned the wheel.
I would try to drift through it.
It wasn't possible.
But I would try.
Then.
Right there.
The turn.
Rubber off the pavement.
Wheels, airborne.
Flipping in the air.
The trees twisting around me.
The sky below me.
The ground above me.
A watercolor of green and blue.
Tumbling.
And tumbling.
And tumbling.
Moving so fast around me.
Forming into something else.
A crowd.
People cheering with signs.
Buildings.
Boats docked.
This was the Monaco Grand Prix.
The greatest place to be in Formula One.
But I had crashed.

My F1 car spinning in the air.

Tearing itself to pieces.

The fans awaiting a tragedy.

Cameras flickering in unison like the light of a lone candle dancing against the wind of the night.

The crash frozen in time on each click . . . each flash.

Flash!

Flash!

Flash!

And there's the picture.

There's the headline image.

My F1 car spiraling in the air.

Tearing to pieces.

In all its glory.

The life and death of a Formula One driver taking it past the limit.

Finally, coming back down to Earth.

Flames.

Heat.

Smoke.

Stillness.

The white clouds blow through.

The red all around you disperses.

And hands pull you out.

"Oh my God," someone said. "His eyes are opening. Look. Look!"

A silhouette hovered over me, and I could tell from its touch it was Tori.

"Tori," I moaned.

"Yes, yes, it's Tori."

"Where am I?" I asked.

"The hospital."

She held my hand.

"Stay put, Osk," she said. "We don't want you to hurt yourself."

The doctor came in. I didn't recognize him.

"Can you hear me, Oscar?" he asked.

"Ye . . ." I tried.

Then Tori's hand slipped from me, and I was tumbling in the air. The force of the spinning was starting to make me lose consciousness. I could feel myself drifting from this life.

"No, no, no, no!" I heard from very far away. "What's happening to him?"

I felt something pushing against my chest.

I heard panic.

Then I heard . . .

Nothing.

I went into that Victorian house for the last time. I went up the stairs and into the bedrooms. I thought up nothing but silence as I dragged my weakened soul against the creaking floors. There was no music. No "Lacrimosa" by Mozart playing in my mind as I imagined would've happened. Because I knew this day would come and I thought about the end every morning after my father blew up and my mother gave herself to drugs. And this end was now, and I wanted it. And my mind was silent. And I did what my grandmother always did when she left the places she loved.

"Come on," I said, waving my hands to guide the memories out of the rooms. "Time to leave," I said. I did this in each room. Then I made my way back down to the first floor and I went into the living room and the dining room and then into the kitchen. Much had happened in that kitchen. There were so many memories to wave out and bring with me. And, after I gathered all of them, I would not go out the front door. I would only go out through the back. Because it made it less of the end that way. Like I wasn't fully leaving somehow. You should never exit through the front door when you leave your home for good. I learned that from my grandmother. And now I knew what she really meant by it. Finally, I understood what she meant about a lot of things. It's amazing how the advice of an older person needs to age with you for you to understand it. So, I shut that back door behind me and inhaled that country breeze like I was taking my last gulp of air.

I would bottle up these memories now and I would wear them around my neck as some type of ornamentation. I would look ahead beyond this house behind me. I would walk toward those woods of my unknown future. And I would hold these memories tight to my chest, thinking about what was lost because I'd only focused on what had been lost. I would think on this on my way into those woods. I would think on it. And think on it. And think on it. And the weight of the memories around my neck made me go slower and slower and slower. I could barely breathe now. Each step made me sink deeper and deeper and deeper into the ground.

I could wear these memories no longer. They were too heavy for me. So, I tore at the rope from which they hung. It took a few tries, but eventually they fell to the earth and into a thousand pieces. But nothing spilled. And that's when I realized I hadn't taken a thing from that house. Because it was all a lie. Perfection isn't in the thing that is lost; perfection is in the thing that never was—the geometry of the memory. The thing that holds you back. "Fuck it," I said. I would walk into those woods into my future. I would walk into what could have been because nothing had ever been. And, so, I did. Until I stopped at the edge of the woods. I watched the madness of the branches, those craggy sinewed curling trees making their way up into the dripping light of the fog-cloaked moon. I heard those 3.0-litre V-10 engines in there somewhere, moaning like an angered cat, sweeping through the air as clean as bullets. Eight hundred horsepower.

Revving to 17,500 rpm. I heard the fans in that collective roar. Their total awe of my talent. Tori was in there somewhere. My kids were in there somewhere. I could see the spotlights of the circuit in there somewhere. It was all in there somewhere. What could've been. The memory of what hadn't ever been.

So, I walked in, and I had my red-and-white Marlboro racing suit on. The fans all around me. Those lights all around me. My teammates spraying me with an oversized G. H. Mumm champagne bottle. Celebrating my seventh world title. I was the greatest racecar driver of all time.

I could hear through the crowd's praise someone calling my name from afar. They were crying out and begging me to wake up. "Wake up! Wake up!" they pleaded. Unlike before, I paid more attention to these slight sounds and I grasped at them and held onto them, finally escaping from that smokescreen of distraction around me. It was just me and the subtlety of another world I'd always ignored.

I could now hear the crisp steady beeping of an EKG, which set the pace of "He Stopped Loving Her Today" by George Jones. I could see a man in a white coat sweeping his flashlight over my eyes. I could feel a warm tear trickle down my cheek.

"Oh, my God," I whispered to myself.

There she was.

Through the muddied vision of my crying eyes there was the blurred silhouette of Tori.

She approached me.

Hovered over me.

And I felt her embrace.

But the crowd broke this intimate calm.

They began to chant my name, "Osk! Osk! Osk!"

Eclipsing the *Beep. Beep. Beep.*

Which to follow?

Which?

But I knew.

I always really knew.
There's only one way to build a future now.
"Osk!"
I would hear and see and feel for the last time.
"Osk!"
So, I smiled up at Tori.
"Osk!"
And I raised my trembling hand to her face.
"Osk!"
And then I closed my eyes.
"Osk!"
And I walked away in that red-and-white Marlboro racing suit.
"Osk!"
"Osk!"
"Osk!"
And I raised my arm in victory as it fell against the bed.

www.ingramcontent.com/pod-product-compliance
Lightning Source LLC
LaVergne TN
LVHW041936070526
838199LV00051BA/2811